THE BILLIONAIRE
BRIDE TEST

ELLE JAMES

TWISTED PAGE INC

THE BILLIONAIRE BRIDE TEST

BILLIONAIRE ONLINE DATING SERVICE BOOK #3

New York Times & *USA Today*
Bestselling Author

ELLE JAMES

Ebook ISBN: 978-1-62695-038-2

Print ISBN: 978-1-62695-039-9

AUTHOR'S NOTE

Enjoy other billionaire books by Elle James

The Billionaire Husband Test (#1)
The Billionaire Cinderella Test (#2)
The Billionaire Bride Test (#3)
The Billionaire Daddy Test (#4)
The Billionaire Matchmaker Test (#5)

Visit ellejames.com for more titles and release dates
For hot cowboys, visit her alter ego Myla Jackson at
mylajackson.com
and join Elle James and Myla Jackson's Newsletter at
Newsletter

CHAPTER 1

"I CAN'T BELIEVE you dragged us all the way to Vegas for this bachelor party. Couldn't we have settled for 6th Street in Austin? At least there, I know where we can go to blend in," Maxwell Smithson said, looking over the top of his sunglasses at the runway in front of him.

"Moose, Coop is the first of our band of brothers to head into the unknown waters of matrimony," Taggert Bronson said. "We couldn't let him go out with a fizzle."

"That's right," Sean O'Leary said. "Besides, we needed the time away from everything to blow off some steam."

Max shook his head and looked around at the crowded theater. "You call this getting away from it all? I was better off back at my ranch, away from all the noise and paparazzi."

"If you weren't built like a tank," Cooper Johnson said, "you wouldn't have been spotted so easily."

Max slipped his sunglasses back up his nose and stared morosely at the runway in front of him. "You think I *like* being groped by every woman on the strip?"

Gage grinned. "Some men would die to be in your jersey." He clapped a hand on Max's back. "All those beautiful women clamoring to be the next Mrs. Smithson... Coop's found the love of his life. And I've found mine. Isn't it time for you, Sean and Tag to find yours?"

Sean held up a hand. "Hey, leave me out of this. I'm a dyed-in-the-wool, never-gonna-change-me, confirmed bachelor."

Tag nodded. "I will. Soon. But I've got a few things to wrap up before I jump into the fray."

Max had been thinking along those same lines after watching Coop, and then Gage, meet their match and fall in love. He hated to admit it but... "I'm considering it."

Tag pounded Max on the back. "That's great to hear. Leslie will have you profiled so fast you won't know what hit you."

Max frowned. "You're not helping the sales pitch with that line of thinking."

Tag grinned. "Leslie's got this thing down. Didn't she find Coop's gal, Emma? Isn't that why we're here?"

"And she found Fiona for me," Gage said. "I've got no complaints. Fiona's everything I'd ever hoped for, and then some."

"Just because you two were fortunate enough to find someone through her online dating service, doesn't mean I'll have the same luck," Max said. "Besides, I'm not looking for the same kind of women you two found."

His four friends looked at him with raised brows.

"Uh, Moose, old buddy," Sean said, "what other kind of women are there? No, wait. There are other kinds, and I bet you'll find them all here in Vegas."

The others laughed.

Max rolled his eyes behind his sunglasses. "No, I'm sick and tired of beautiful women."

"Seriously?" Sean shook his head. "Since when are beautiful women a bad thing?"

"Since they all seem more interested in how they look than what they bring to the relationship." Max crossed his arms over his chest. "I want a plain woman with simple needs."

"Dude." Sean grimaced. "You're talking about my grandmother."

"Exactly," Max said with a crisp nod. "Someone who doesn't want the limelight, prefers to be at home, and most importantly, wants children and isn't afraid of a few stretch marks getting them." Max held up a hand to keep Sean from poking more fun at him. "But one that's closer to my age. She can

3

even be a little older, as long as she doesn't mind sharing kitchen duty and getting dirty on the ranch."

"What about sexual compatibility?"

Max shrugged. "Sex isn't everything."

"Whoa! Wait just an unholy minute," Sean leaned back, blinking. "I did not hear that coming from my buddy, Moose."

Max cocked an eyebrow. "Lasting respect is."

Gage shook his head. "Sexual compatibility is very important. Think about it; the woman you marry is the last person you'll have sex with for the rest of your life. If you can't get it up for her, you're screwed. And I don't mean in a good way."

"Yeah." Max pressed his lips together. "Sex is important, but I'd rather focus on liking the person I spend the rest of my life with. I've seen people marry who are in lust with each other. When the lust wears off, they have nothing left to keep them together." He lifted is chin. "When I marry, I want to grow old with that person."

"But you don't want to be bored out of your mind." Gage shook his head. "I guess I'm lucky. I'm marrying someone who's beautiful inside and out. Someone I'll never grow bored of. You really should give Leslie's dating service a try. I've never been happier."

"Same goes for me," Coop said, his eyes a little glassy from over-consumption of alcohol. "Emma's the best. I would never have found her without BODS."

"And what's up with that name, BODS?" Max asked. "Who names a dating service BODS?"

"She named it for people like us," Tag said and looked around to see if anyone was listening to them. "You remember what the B stands for…" He leaned closer to Max and whispered, "Billionaire."

"I know what the B stands for, but how many billionaires are out there who need an online dating service?"

"Probably more than you think," Coop said. "I'm just glad I was able to find the love of my life through Leslie's service." He grinned. "And I'm marrying her in two short weeks."

"Shh, the show's about to start," Sean said and nodded his head to the announcer stepping out on the runway.

"And that's another thing," Max said. "Whose idea was it to book a lingerie modeling show for a bachelor party?"

"It was the closest thing I could book to a stripper that met with Emma's approval," Tag said. "She told me absolutely no strippers. It was this or a drag queen show."

"Hey, you don't see me complaining," Sean said. "Bring on the pretty girls in bras and panties."

Max braced himself for an hour or more of women parading down an elevated runway in nothing more than their undergarments. Not that he didn't appreciate scantily clad ladies, but these weren't ladies he wanted to take home. And he was ready for someone he *wanted* to take home.

"What exactly are you looking for in a woman?" Tag asked.

Max tilted his head to one side and thought. "You know, as a retired NFL football player, I've had more than my share of scantily-clad women showing up uninvited in my hotel room, apartment and house. All were beautiful and brainless, and they starved themselves so thin I felt like I could snap them in two, like a twig."

"I dated one like that," Sean said. "Kind of scary. I felt like I could break her in half, making love to her."

Max nodded. "Right. What I want is a woman who isn't afraid of gaining a pound. Someone who doesn't mind getting dirt under her fingernails. A lady who can wear cowboy boots and, even if she doesn't know how to ride a horse, is willing to learn. And she must have a brain. No airheads."

"What if she's smarter than you?" Tag asked. "Will that challenge your masculinity?"

Max shook his head. "Not in the least. I want someone who challenges me intellectually."

"Wow, you don't want much out of your match," Tag said. "All I want is someone who wants me, not my money."

Max pointed to Tag. "That, too."

"Be sure to have your list ready when you go see Leslie," Tag said. "She'll find that match for you. Her system is amazing."

Max crossed his arms over his chest. He'd be the judge of that. The first two matches could have been pure luck. He wouldn't be convinced until he found his match. Until then...

The show started with an announcement of the outfit being worn—or what there was of it—and the model strutting her stuff in impossibly high heels. And she had on some crazy pink butterfly wings that were taller than she was. And she was tall. The skimpy panties and bra barely covered her hoo-hah and nipples, and she had on enough makeup to sink a ship.

What was wrong with these women? Didn't they realize how ridiculous they looked? What Max wouldn't give for a wholesome country girl, farm-raised and makeup-free.

He held his breath until the model made it to the end of the runway, turned and started back.

Max didn't breathe again until she'd made it safely back to the curtain. "How in the world do they do that?"

Sean chuckled. "Do what?"

"Walk on those stilts?" Max shook his head. "It's a wonder they don't fall and break their fool necks."

"You see? How can you knock them? Beautiful women work hard at being beautiful. It isn't easy walking in those shoes or with those wings attached to their backs. It takes talent," Sean said. "Like this one." He nodded toward the next model wearing a white bra and panties set trimmed in gold. She wore an elaborate set of angel wings on her back decorated with fluffy white ostrich feathers. Those ostrich feathers wafted toward her face. One, in particular, seemed to be loose and holding on by a string of glue. It floated beneath the model's nose.

Max had to give the woman credit; she kept her face steady for the entire walk down the long runway. When she spun, the feather swung out.

For a moment, Max thought it would settle behind her.

Alas, with each step, it floated closer to her face until it was back beneath her nose.

At that moment, she was passing where Max and his friends stood.

His fingers itched to pluck the feather from beneath her nose. Though he was tall, the runway was elevated and too high for him to reach up and help her out.

The feather did its damage.

The woman's nose wrinkled first, then her chest heaved, and she let loose a suppressed sneeze. The force of the act rocked her on her high heels. She flung out her arms and fell. Down, down, down, as if in slow motion.

As with football, when Max saw something

coming his way, he reached out to catch it. Since he was the tallest of his group, it made sense for him to catch the falling model.

She tumbled backward, landing in Max's outstretched arms, angel wings and all.

The crowd gasped in horror. A camera flashed in Max's sunglasses-covered eyes.

Sean, Coop, Tag and Gage surrounded him, protecting him from the paparazzi.

When he had her firmly in his grasp, Max stared down through the ostrich feathers into the prettiest violet eyes. Her hair had been slicked back so tightly, he couldn't tell if she was blond, brunette, black or red-haired.

Her slender arm draped over his shoulder, the tips of her fingers touching his ear.

"Thank you," she said. "You saved me."

He snorted. "If you didn't wear such insanely high heels, you wouldn't have fallen."

"Tell me about it," she said. "Help me back up. I have to get back to work."

He set her on her feet.

She stared at the runway, four feet above where she stood. Then she glanced around, as if looking for an exit.

"Need help getting back up there?" Max asked.

She glanced back at him with a small grimace and a nod. "I'll manage."

No way would she find her way through the crowd.

Before she could turn away, he lifted her off her feet.

She let out a little squeal and clung to his shoulders as he set her on the stage.

Once she had her feet firmly on the platform, she rose above him and straightened on those impossibly high heels.

Mouthing the words, *Thank you*, she spun on those heels and walked back down the runway to the clapping hands of the crowd happy to see she wasn't injured and could finish her circuit. If her wings were a little lopsided, no one seemed to care.

Sean pounded Max on the back. "You might not need Leslie's online dating service after all. Wish I could be so lucky as to have the woman of my dreams land in my lap like that."

Max's gaze followed the woman down the runway until she disappeared behind the velvet curtain. Though she'd felt good in his arms, and her violet eyes had been amazing... "She's not my type."

"Dude," Tag said. "She's a female with a rockin' body. She's *every* man's type."

"Right?" Sean said. "Did you at least get her number?"

"No." Max gave Sean a frowning glance. "I told you, I want a woman who isn't so into her looks she's afraid to eat a hamburger." Although the model had

had curves in all the right places, she'd been too beautiful. And beautiful women, in his experience, didn't stick around. They were more interested in themselves than a lasting relationship. "Man, if you'd wanted her number so much, you should have caught her."

Max stared up at the stage as the next model came out, wearing a set of gold filigree wings and a matching gold bikini. She was even thinner than the one he'd held in his arms. His gaze went to the curtain where the violet-eyed beauty had disappeared. Would she be out again in another outfit?

Max had been ready to leave the show and go back to their suite of rooms to drink a couple of beers and call it a night. But after catching the angel-winged beauty, his interest had been captured. He stayed, hoping to catch another glimpse of those eyes.

Unfortunately, she didn't reappear after her first disastrous trek down the runway. Or, if she had, he didn't recognize her in whatever crazy outfit she'd worn next. From the distance, he couldn't pick out eye color.

The night ended when Coop excused himself to call his fiancée.

"I have a beer with my name on it back at the suite. You're welcome to join me," Max said to the others.

Gage nodded. "I'm all for a beer."

"We can't desert the groom," Tag said.

Sean sighed. "Remind me not to fall in love. It takes all the fun out of playing the field."

Tag looped an arm over Sean's shoulders. "When you fall in love, you won't care about playing the field."

"All the more reason to remain single," Sean said. "Let's go. I could use some whiskey."

With one last glance at the runway, in search of the violet-eyed model, Max hooked Coop's elbow and led him through the throng of people.

Coop cupped his cellphone to his ear as he tried to talk with Emma over the roar of the crowd.

The man was besotted.

For the first time in his life, Max found himself envious of his friend and even more eager to give Leslie's Billionaire Online Dating Service a chance. What could it hurt? Either it worked, or it didn't. He had to try.

JANE GENTRY RUBBED her ankle in the dressing room. She wasn't sure how she'd made it back down the runway after her fall, but now that she was off the heels, she couldn't stand in them again. She was done for the night. One of the other models would have to fill in for her.

Her skin still tingled from where the big man in the crowd had held her. She wished she'd gotten his name so that she could call and thank him again for saving her from breaking her neck.

A twisted ankle was much better than a broken neck.

The entire incident brought it home to her, even more clearly, that it was time for her to retire from the modeling scene.

She didn't need the money. Her modeling career had taken off early in her life, and she'd invested wisely, amassing a fortune of her own. Over the past few years, she'd been very selective about the gigs she'd accepted. She'd only agreed to this one in Vegas as a favor for a friend, and because all the money generated from ticket sales would go toward the local children's hospital.

Beyond this engagement, she had only one more in Dallas in a few weeks and she was done. Again, if it wasn't a charity event, she'd have cancelled that one as well.

One of the assistants helped her out of the wings and costume and into her own street clothes. Jane called the car service, located an icepack and applied it to her ankle while she waited. In flats, she was able to hobble out to the car and get inside without help. Before long, she was back at her hotel, packing her bag for her trip back to Austin in her home state of Texas.

When she was ready and had scheduled a car for the trip to the airport in the morning, Jane lay in the king-size bed, staring up at the hotel ceiling. Sleep, as usual, was hard to come by.

Since she was ten, she'd been on the treadmill of modeling gigs. Almost twenty years. With her thirtieth birthday bearing down on her, she had begun to question her career choice and her future.

Over the past twenty years, with the guidance of her parents and financial advisors, she'd done very well. Investments of her earnings from modeling, sponsorships, a clothing and a perfume line, had grown to the point she didn't have to work another day in her life, and she'd never spend all the money she had. But what, besides money, did she have to show for it all?

She had no doubt the girls she'd gone to grade school with, had she kept up with them, had all married and had a couple of kids by now. Their worries would be what to pack in school lunch boxes and what to cook for dinner, while balancing a career.

Jane loved to cook but rarely had the opportunity to do so. And whatever she cooked couldn't pass her lips for fear she'd gain a pound or two.

What she wouldn't give for a cheeseburger with all the fixings. She sighed. For as long as she'd been modeling, cheeseburgers had been taboo.

She found her thoughts going back to the man who'd caught her. He'd worn sunglasses, so she hadn't gotten a good look at his face. But those hands... They'd been big, coarse and strong. The chest she'd landed against had been rock solid. A man like that could protect her from the paparazzi and make love to her like nobody's business. And he'd make strong babies for her to love and hold.

She wished she'd gotten his number.

Jane closed her eyes, a plan forming.

It was time to retire from modeling and start the next chapter of her life. She'd put living and loving on hold, but time was running out if she wanted the whole enchilada.

Her mouth watered at the thought of eating a whole enchilada. When was the last time she'd eaten dinner without counting a single calorie? Too long!

Last time she'd been in Austin, she'd run into one of the only friends she'd kept in touch with from grade school, Leslie Lambert. Hadn't she said she was developing an online dating service just for people who wanted the safety, security and individual attention needed to navigate the dating world? Leslie had said she personally screened all potential candidates prior to allowing them to enter her system.

Was it possible that Leslie could find Jane a fella just right for her?

She wanted someone who didn't care if she gained a pound or two. Someone who would love her without knowing how much money she had in the bank. A man with big hands and strong muscles.

A man like the one whose arms she'd fallen into from the runway...

When she got back to Austin, she'd look up Leslie, bring her list of requirements and start the search for her perfect match.

For the first time in a long time, Jane fell asleep with a smile on her face and hope in her heart. She was ready to embrace the next chapter of her life. Bring it on!

CHAPTER 2

ONCE HE GOT BACK to Austin, Max didn't waste any time making an appointment with Leslie Lambert of the Billionaire Online Dating Service. The problem was, his friends all felt it necessary to join him at his initial consultation.

He didn't like it, but he figured it was fair since he'd been at Coop's and Gage's first meetings with the matchmaker.

But he'd be damned if he let them into the computer room where he'd fill out his questionnaire. That would be all on him.

"So, Moose, what are you going to ask for?" Sean said. "Blonde, redhead, brunette?"

"I don't really care," Max responded. "As long as she's not too pretty. A Plain Jane will suit me just fine."

Tag frowned. "Remember, that could be the face you look at across the table for the rest of your life."

"Then she'll be perfectly satisfied, knowing I didn't marry her for her looks."

Sean winced. "I wouldn't put it to her like that. Most women like to think they're beautiful in their lover's eyes."

"And she will be," Max assured him. "I'll want her to know I value her for her intellect and sense of humor, more than her beauty. Beauty doesn't last."

"What else do you have on your list?" Tag asked.

Max resisted the urge to pat his pocket where he'd shoved the piece of paper he'd used to jot down his wants and desires in a mate. "Who said I made a list?"

"We all have a mental list of the type of woman we think we prefer," Coop said. "I had one in my head when I filled out the questionnaire."

"What did you have on your list?" Max asked, wondering if he should add more to his requirements.

"Let me think..." Sean touched a finger to his chin. "She had to have all her own teeth."

Max frowned. He hadn't thought of that. He wanted a woman who wasn't beautiful, but tooth-less...? He supposed he could afford to help the love of his life get implants.

"I listed the important things, like 'must want children, must love animals and the outdoors'.

Things I enjoy. The experts say opposites attract, but if you want a relationship to last, you have to have more in common than not."

Max nodded.

"Come on, Moose," Sean elbowed him in the side. "Spill. We want to know what you can't live without in a woman."

Max shook his head. "No way. If you ever meet the woman...not that I'm likely to bring her anywhere close to the likes of all of you...I don't want her to run screaming in the other direction because one of you slips and tells her what's on my list."

Tag clapped a hand to his chest. "Hey, you can trust me."

"I might be able to trust some of you, but others —*Sean*—have big mouths." Max sat straighter as the door to the conference room opened.

Leslie Lambert, dressed in a stylish gray suit and soft pink blouse, sailed in with a smile. "Well, I didn't expect the entire gang to show up for the third time."

"Shouldn't these yahoos leave?" Max suggested.

Leslie waved a hand. "Not at all. As long as you're comfortable with them being here..."

Max frowned at his friends. "If I say I'm not, will they leave?"

Sean crossed his arms over his chest and shook his head.

Coop grinned. "Not a chance."

"I'm staying." Tag tipped his head toward the woman. "Moral support for Leslie."

"You all watched me as I suffered through the embarrassment," Gage said. "I wouldn't miss Moose's for the world."

The four men Max had once considered his friends all sat back in their conference room chairs with smirks on their faces.

"Might as well get this over with," Max said. "What do you want me to do?"

"I can give you the spiel again, or you can come with me, and we can get right down to finding your match."

Max barely stopped himself from snorting. Though two of his friends had found their matches, he wasn't convinced he'd find his using a computer software program. However, given that he was thirty-four years old and hadn't found the love of his life, he was ready to try anything. He wasn't getting any younger, and he wanted what was missing in his life. A partner and children.

"Let's do this," he said and followed Leslie out of the conference room.

"Good luck, Moose," Coop called out.

"Make good choices," Gage added.

"Remember, that's the face you might have to look at for the rest of your life," Sean said. "Don't go for ugly."

"Shut up, O'Leary," Moose muttered. "I know what I want."

"You say you do, but do you really?" Sean's voice called out, his words echoing down the hallway.

"All you have to do is answer the questionnaire honestly, and the program does the rest," Leslie reassured him.

"Got it," he said, though he would withhold judgement until he saw the questions.

"I have another client in the room right now, but she should be finishing up by now." Leslie paused with her hand on the door to a room several yards down the hallway from the conference room. "Wait here while I check to see if she's done."

She slipped inside.

Curious, Max tried to see who was in the room. If Leslie's other client was filling out the questionnaire, she could be the woman the program matched him with.

Max's heart slammed against his ribs. The woman in the room could be the future Mrs. Maxwell Smithson.

He clenched his suddenly sweating hands into fists and willed his pulse to slow. The fight or flight instinct kicked in, urging him to turn and run. But Moose Smithson never ran from a challenge. He met it head on.

Squaring his shoulders, he drew in a deep breath

and waited for the two women to emerge from the room.

Then a thought occurred to him. If this woman was the one destined to be his future wife, how would she feel seeing him at his pathetic worst, standing in line at a matchmaking firm?

The door handle turned.

Max turned his back to the door and slipped his ever-ready sunglasses over his eyes. He couldn't disguise his size, but the sunglasses made him feel a little less recognizable to the general public.

A woman backed out of the room, wearing a floaty white dress that swirled around her trim calves. Her hair was a sandy-blond and fell straight down her back to a straight line between her shoulder blades. She spoke softly to Leslie who emerged a moment later, smiling.

"I'll be in touch as soon as I know something."

The woman turned, ducked her head and walked past Max without lifting her head.

From what he could tell, she wasn't wearing any makeup, and her facial features were nondescript.

He wished he could have seen her eyes, but they were hidden effectively behind large, round-lensed sunglasses.

Were they violet, like those belonging to the model he'd caught in Vegas? Why he couldn't get that woman out of his mind, he didn't know. She wasn't the kind of woman he pictured himself with for the rest of his life. He'd dated too many beautiful women, and they'd all had one thing in common…they were only interested in themselves, not a relationship with anyone else. Their lives revolved around them as if they were the center of the universe.

"I'll be right back," Leslie murmured as she passed Max. She followed the woman to the exit and shook her hand. Once the client had departed, Leslie turned her smile onto Max and joined him in front of the fated doorway. "Ready?"

Hell no.

Max opened the door and swept out a hand. "Lead the way." He put on a front of nonchalance while inside, his heart was racing, and he thought he might throw up. He hadn't been this nervous since his first time playing quarterback for his NFL team. Back then, all eyes had been on him to perform. Now, he was on his own. No one was judging him, but he felt like what he was about to do could change his life forever.

Leslie pulled out a chair in front of a computer terminal. "Have a seat, Mr. Smithson."

"Max," he corrected.

She nodded. "Max. The questionnaire will take approximately thirty minutes. Take your time, think about your responses and be honest with yourself." She walked to a small refrigerator in the corner and pulled out a plastic bottle of water. "This might help relax you."

"A beer would be better," he said, wishing he had one to get through the next thirty minutes of hell.

Leslie's expression didn't change as she turned to the refrigerator again, pulling out a longneck bottle of beer. "I try to keep a variety of drinks on hand." She popped off the cap and set it on the table beside him.

"You think of everything," he murmured and tipped the bottle up, taking a long draw off the contents before he set it back on the table, half empty.

"I try to." She leaned over the keyboard and rested her hand on the mouse. With three quick clicks, she had the questionnaire loaded. "Click on the boxes on the screen. They're self-explanatory."

"You mean, idiot-proof."

She laughed. "No. That's not what I meant. But do think through your answers and be clear concerning your wants, needs and desires." She straightened. "Can I get you anything else before you start?"

"An escape route?" he quipped.

Leslie laughed. "You don't have to do this. But I think you will be satisfied with the results. If you feel at any time that you don't want to continue to be a part of the system, hit the cancel button at the top of the page. If you don't save it at the end, it doesn't add you to the pool of clients."

Good. If he decided he wasn't ready to start dating strangers, he had an out. That made him feel better. He could go through the questions, see if they made any sense and still have the opportunity to nix the entire plan.

"I'll leave you to it," Leslie said softly and left the room, closing the door with a soft snick behind him.

Alone in the room with the computer, the monitor and no one else, Max placed his hand on the mouse.

Was it still warm from the woman's hand that had been on it before him?

A strange surge of electricity rippled through him.

Max moved the mouse, positioning the cursor of the button on the screen that read, START HERE.

His heart pounded and his hand froze on the mouse. It was as if his life was about to start with those words.

Max shook his head. It was just a computer monitor and a software program. He took his list from his pocket and unfolded it on the table beside him.

Filling out a questionnaire wouldn't change anything. Going on a date wouldn't change anything.

Unless she was the one…

If he was honest with himself, his hand shook just a little as he clicked the mouse, launching him into the questionnaire.

The questionnaire was all about who Max Smith was. He sure as hell wasn't going to use his real name.

Maxwell Smithson, the Moose, NFL football player, was too well known to the media and just about everyone in the U.S. He wanted to meet a woman who wanted to go out with him based on his personal profile, not his media profile.

He filled in all the usual stuff about height, weight, hair color and eye color.

For occupation, he couldn't say NFL football player. He'd retired from that. Now that he wasn't playing, he considered himself a rancher. Did women like ranchers? Or would they consider them too sweaty and dirty?

A smile curled the corners of his lips. Like playing football wasn't dirty and sweaty...

When it came to his preferences, he answered honestly that he preferred the outdoors and rural settings. He didn't like crowds and liked more one-on-one time. Bars weren't his scene, picnics were. Hiking over museums. Staring at the stars versus going to a movie.

Though he was smart and had invested wisely, he preferred to work with his hands rather than with his brain. He'd rather put in a hard day's work hauling hay over sitting in an office chair any day. Unless it was a typical one-hundred-degree day in Texas. Then he might prefer to hang out in his pool. But the questionnaire didn't have that as an option.

Did he like animals? Max snorted. If he didn't, he wouldn't have three dogs, five horses and a barnyard full of the typical critters, like chickens, pigs and goats. Yes, he liked animals. He glanced at his list. That was top on his list for the woman he hoped to meet. She had to like animals.

And food. She couldn't be one of those bone-thin models he'd seen in Vegas. He wanted a woman who knew how to throw down a cheeseburger and wasn't afraid of getting dirty.

Max met page after page of questions with his answers, until he thought the computer knew more about him than even his mother.

After he'd finished entering all his data, he clicked the CONTINUE button and waited, expecting the monitor to display his requirements for the woman he wanted to meet.

A smiley face emoji appeared on the screen and the words QUESTIONNAIRE COMPLETE displayed on the monitor.

"What the hell?" He clicked the back button. The hourglass indicated the program was thinking and working. When it was done, the monitor displayed WELCOME TO BODS.

Max hit enter and the START HERE appeared on the screen.

"You've got to be kidding me." He pushed back his chair, glanced at his watch and headed for the door. Had he really been sitting there for thirty minutes and only finished describing his preferences about *himself*?

As he reached for the doorknob, it twisted, and Leslie popped her head through the gap in the door. "All done?"

Max frowned. "I'm not sure."

Leslie smiled. "Why?"

"I only answered questions about me. Wasn't I supposed to have a place to enter my preferences for the woman I hope to meet?"

Leslie's smile widened. "By answering the questionnaire about yourself, you did that."

Max shook his head. "I have an entire list of things I want in a woman."

Leslie nodded. "I'm sure you do. Based on the answers to your questions, the program will select the woman who most fits your personality."

"But don't I have a say in whether she's a blonde or brunette?"

Leslie patted his arm. "Does hair color really matter?" Leslie laid a hand against his chest. "What matters is who you are and who she is inside." She looked into his eyes. "Trust me, my system will find your perfect match."

Max gritted his teeth. He liked to be in control of his life. Everything about the BODS system made him feel like he was not the one in control. He didn't like that at all.

"Max, it'll be all right." Leslie patted his arm. "You don't have to marry the woman if you don't like her."

"Who said anything about marriage?" Max said, his voice tight. "As far as I'm concerned, I'm going on one date. If things don't work out, that will be the only date."

The light in Leslie's eyes twinkled, and her lips twitched as if she were holding back a smile. "All I ask is that you keep an open mind. If a date is all you want, a date is all you'll get." She raised an eyebrow. "I screen all my clients."

"I hope you do. I'd hate to think you cater to crooks, thieves or felons."

"You don't understand." Her lips pressed together, and she poked a finger at his chest. "I screen all of them. Including you." She dropped her arm to her side.

"Will my match know all about me?"

She shook her head. "Only what you chose to tell her on your questionnaire."

"She won't know how much money I have in the bank or that I played NFL football?"

"Not if you didn't put it in the questionnaire."

"I didn't use all of my name," he said. "It would've been a dead giveaway."

Leslie frowned. "What name did you use?"

"Max Smith, instead of Maxwell Smithson or Moose."

She nodded. "I suppose that's all right. It's close enough without being exact." Her frown cleared. "I guess you're done then."

"Wait. What about my preferences in the woman?"

"As I said, the computer will match based on your likes and dislikes. The program works. Give it a chance." She herded him toward the conference room where his buddies were waiting.

Max felt as if he was swimming against the current and no amount of muscle was going to get him out of the flow.

Leslie opened the door to the conference room and gave him a gentle shove, propelling him inside. "He's all yours. You might take him for a beer. I think he's bordering on a full-on panic attack." With a wink, she added, "Really, Max, you're going to be all right. Trust me. Now, if you'll excuse me, I have to run a program."

"How long will it take to find Moose's match?" Sean asked. "We can't wait to see what you come up with."

"Not what," she corrected. "Who. And it shouldn't take long at all. But it will take a day or two for the parties involved to agree to a time and place for the first date." She pinned Max with a pointed stare. "Be thinking about it. You can only make a first impression once." Then she was gone.

Tag pushed to his feet. "I think I'll go help her."

"She needs help?" Max ran a hand through his hair, his pulse hammering through his veins.

Tag waggled his eyebrows. "No, but you know

me. I like computers." He glanced at the other men. "Let me know where you'll be if you decide to take the man out for a beer."

"By the panicked look on Moose's face, there will be beer," Cooper said with a chuckle.

"We'll text the location once we get there," Sean said. "Let us know what she comes up with, will ya?"

Tag frowned. "I can't do that. Names are confidential to the clients. If the woman selected agrees to a date, Moose is the only one who will know." He turned toward Moose. "We'll expect full disclosure when you find out who she is."

Moose snorted. "Only if I agree to the date as well."

"Oh, you'll agree," Tag said with assurance. "BODS knows you better than you know yourself."

"Put your money where your mouth is, Tag," Moose shot back. "Let BODS find your perfect match."

"I told you, I have a few things to wrap up before I take the plunge. But I will. I trust Leslie and her program to find my perfect woman." He left the room, hurrying after Leslie.

"Well, that leaves us to drag your ass to a bar and get you shitfaced." Sean pushed to his feet. "Let's do this, before you come unglued. You're looking a little shell-shocked."

"I just signed up for a blind date," Max said, shaking his head and feeling a little woozy on his feet. "You remember the last blind date I went on? It did not end well."

Coop laughed. "You mean, you didn't enjoy your date with Candy Schepanski? What was she, six-feet-four inches with a voice that would make fingernails on a chalkboard sound like a lullaby?"

"Her height wasn't so bad, and I could have put up with the voice, but she was absolutely psycho," Max said. "She thought one dinner and a movie made us a couple. It took me a full year of avoiding her before she finally quit stalking me."

"I remember," Gage said. "You couldn't step out of your apartment without running into her. Didn't she crawl through your window and surprise you by stripping naked and lying in your bed, waiting for you to get home from football practice?"

Max nodded. "It got so bad, I had to move with no forwarding address—and she still found me. I didn't have a life for that entire year. I couldn't go anywhere but class, practice and games."

Gage's eyes narrowed. "Who set you up with her?"

Max turned to Sean. "You set me up with her. You said she was a tall, gorgeous drink of water, and I should get to know her."

Sean held up his hands. "She was a tall, gorgeous drink of water. How was I to know she would turn stalker on you?"

Max glared at his friend. "I still owe you for that one.

"It's been ten years," Sean said. "You should be over it by now."

"I'm having flashbacks." Max spun toward the door. "I'm calling this off. I can't do this."

Coop grabbed his elbow. "Time for that beer. Everything will be okay. Things will work out." He led him out into the hall.

Gage gripped his other arm. Between his two friends, he was hustled out of the building and into Coop's truck. The other three men climbed in, and they set off to find one of their favorite Austin watering holes, where they could get a beer without being hounded by the paparazzi.

Max sat in the front passenger seat, with what felt like a permanent frown scrunching his face. "What about my truck?"

"You won't be in any condition to drive after we're done with you."

"Shouldn't I remain sober?" Max had been in some pretty tight situations on the football field, but he'd never felt as out of control as he was at that moment. "What if Leslie calls me with my match? What kind of first impression will I make if I slur my words?"

"It won't happen that fast," Gage said. "She'll contact the woman, first. If the woman agrees to see you, she'd contact you next. You'll have time to sober up. Right now, you need to relax."

Max drew in a deep breath. "I could relax on my ranch and be perfectly happy."

"Yeah, but we wouldn't be around to enjoy watching you lose your shit." Sean laughed and clapped him on the back from his position in the backseat of the truck. "I don't think I've ever seen the Moose this tightly wound."

"I'm not wound," Max said.

"The hell you're not," Gage said. "I want to be there when you get the call."

"Me, too." Sean said. "I say we camp out at Moose's ranch until it comes."

"I'd love to be there, too," Coop said, "but I'm getting married in less than two weeks. I'm thinking Emma will have me running errands and tying up loose ends until the big day."

"Yeah, and I haven't invited any of you to camp out at the ranch," Max said. "Unless you come prepared to work. I just did a cutting of hay. You can help me get it into the barn tomorrow and the next day." Max turned in his seat, his brow raised. "Well? Any takers?"

Sean held up his hands. "I just remembered; I left the iron on in my penthouse."

"And I have to help Coop with his wedding errands," Gage said.

"Yeah." Max crossed his arms over his chest. "Thought so. Well, if you free up, you know where I'll be. And I won't be waiting around for the phone to ring."

"Damned shame," Sean muttered. "I'd love to see how you handle it."

"Me, too," Gage said.

"I'll handle it just fine," Max assured them. "On my own time. After I'm done in the field."

"Have you thought about where you'll take her on the first date?" Coop asked.

Max nodded. "I have. I'm taking her out to the ranch."

"Holy shit." Sean leaned forward. "You're not going to make her haul hay, are you?"

"No, dumbass." His lips twisted. "But I want to know she can handle ranch life."

"That's right. You want a woman who isn't afraid to get dirty." Sean sat back. "On a first date?"

Gage shook his head. "You're doomed."

Max's jaw tightened. "I also want to know she's up for any adventure. She has to be spontaneous and flexible."

"On your first date?" Coop also shook his head. "You're supposed to impress her by taking her to a nice restaurant and bringing her flowers, not taking her out to the barn to shovel horse manure."

Sean reached out and knocked on Max's head. "Are you sure you didn't get hit once too often and suffer some traumatic brain injury?"

Max shoved Sean's hand away. "No, I did not. I want to know from the get-go that she's the kind of woman who isn't afraid of a challenge. If she's not up to it on the first date, I see no reason for a second date."

Sean clapped his palm to his forehead. "Doomed, I tell you."

"Shut up. I'm not going to be a complete jerk," Max said. "I'll wine and dine her...but I'll do it my way. Now, take me back to my truck. I have work to do before I meet Leslie's pick. You all are welcome to join me. I pay in beer...when the hay is safely stored in the barn."

"Moose, you have enough money to pay someone to haul your hay," Coop pointed out. "Why are you still doing it?"

Max straightened and tipped up his chin. "I like to be reminded where I came from. We didn't always have it so easy."

Coop nodded. "I remember hauling hay in the summer to earn money so we could eat during the fall semester at Texas A&M." He glanced at his cell phone. "Let me give Emma a call. If she doesn't have anything on our agenda for today and tomorrow, I'll help."

Gage nodded. "What kind of beer are you offering?"

"Whatever kind you want." Max grinned.

"Well, damn." Sean sighed. "I guess you all are going to shame me into hauling hay with you." He gave a chin lift. "I'm in. But I want Guinness—none of that cheap shit." He lifted his phone. "I'll text Tag and tell him to bring his work clothes out to your ranch."

They didn't make it to the bar. Instead, they swung back by Leslie's office building and collected Max's truck and Tag. With the whole gang together, they headed out to Max's ranch to haul hay.

The hard work over the next couple of days helped keep Max's mind off the results of the BODS program. But every time his cellphone rang, he jumped, expecting a call from Leslie. By the end of the second day, he was beginning to think there wasn't a perfect woman out there for him.

CHAPTER 3

JANE ONLY HAD to wait until the end of the day before Leslie called to say she'd found a match.

Quietly, she'd thanked Leslie and told her she'd call her back, that she was busy with a project. She'd held herself together until she'd ended the call, and then went into a full-on, meltdown panic attack.

She wasn't ready to date. It was too soon. Somehow, she'd thought it would take days of scouring through potential candidates to come up with one who matched her profile. Not less than four hours!

Since it was the end of the day anyway, Jane put off returning Leslie's call. That night, she didn't sleep at all. Every scenario she came up with for a first date ended badly. He'd pick his nose. She'd drink too much wine. He'd want to get to first base before they had dinner. She'd choke on her salad.

Just how long had it been since she'd been on a date?

She thought back. Other than publicity stunts, she hadn't been on a date in the past five years. And the last one had been a total disaster. The man had been a superstar athlete. She'd thought he would be a safe bet. Athletes trained hard. They had to be disciplined.

Who knew hockey players were so violent in the rink and totally full of themselves? He'd asked her out because she'd been on the cover of *Sports Illustrated Magazine*, modeling a bikini. He'd only wanted the publicity of dating her, not the actual emotional connection.

He'd even scheduled the press to show up at the restaurant he'd taken her to. When the cameras arrived, he'd pulled her into his arms and kissed her in front of everyone.

She'd been so shocked, she hadn't put up much of a fight. But when he'd flirted with the waitresses and didn't talk to her throughout the meal, he'd grated on her last nerve.

Jane had ordered the most expensive dessert on the menu. When the waitress delivered the chocolate lava cake, something Jane would never normally have ordered, she took one bite and dumped the rest of the gooey, syrupy mess over her date's head.

On her way out of the restaurant without him, she'd alerted the press lurking by the door to the condition of the player. They'd surged into the restaurant and photographed the hockey player à la chocolate lava cake.

The media had had a field day with the photos, siding with the hockey player and calling her all kinds of nasty names, like ice princess and psycho model.

The incident hadn't hurt her career at all. In fact, she'd been in even higher demand than before, because everyone wanted to see what the "psycho model" looked like.

Some women cheered her. Others condemned her for attacking the handsome player. Men avoided her. She didn't care. Jane had a growing career, demanding all her attention, until now.

Earlier in the year, her financial advisor had told her that she had enough money saved and royalties coming in from her lines of clothing and perfumes to last her the rest of her life. If she wanted, she could quit modeling.

The idea had taken root and spread.

She could stop starving herself and, finally, eat a hamburger. She could take up cooking and actually eat the food she made. Jane loved to bake and had dreamed of writing her own cookbook.

Now that she'd set her plan in place and had slowly scaled back her commitments, she was ready to get on with living the rest of her life.

She sat on the covered porch of her house in the suburbs of Austin, staring out at the swimming pool she'd only swim in after sunset to keep from getting a sunburn.

Part of getting on with her life was starting to date again. But she wanted to date a real man. Not a cocky, limelight-hungry athlete or movie star. Not into the bar scene, she'd agreed to give her friend Leslie's Billionaire Online Dating Service a try to take the guesswork out of finding a match.

Now that she had...

Nothing was more awkward than sitting across a table, coming up with small talk at a restaurant. Why did dates have to be at restaurants?

Holy hell. She wasn't ready. What would she wear? What would she say? What if she hated him? What if he hated her?

All she had to do was walk away or try again. She couldn't move on with the rest of her life if she didn't take that first step.

What was she waiting for?

She held her cellphone in front of her, her hand shaking as she keyed in her text response to Leslie.

Let's do this

A moment later, her cellphone rang.

"I thought you'd fallen off the face of the earth," Leslie exclaimed. "Let me tell you about him before I tell him about you."

Jane leaned forward, her heart slamming into her ribs. "You're not going to tell him who I am, are you?"

"Not that you're a supermodel. Only about what

you put in your profile. If he's okay with everything, I'll give him the email address we set up through BODS. He'll contact you through it."

"Good. I don't want him to know anything about my modeling life, my businesses or that I have a bank account big enough to buy a state."

Leslie laughed. "It's called the Billionaire Online Dating Service for a reason. My clients want to match with someone based on their own personal merits, not based on their bank accounts."

"Good," Jane said. "Now, give me the goods on my match."

"He's thirty-four years old, blond and blue-eyed, and is six-feet-four inches."

"Good. I can wear heals if I like." Which she didn't, if it wasn't on a runway or a public event, but it would be nice to have the option.

"He likes animals," Leslie continued.

"I had a cat once," Jane said. The cat hadn't liked people and had barely tolerated her. But it was the only pet her mother had let her have growing up. "Go on."

"He likes the outdoors."

Jane stared at the sunshine glinting off the water of her pool. "I like being outside."

"He believes in working hard but taking time off to have fun."

Jane sighed. "I think I'm already in love."

Even though she was giving up modeling, she

knew she couldn't laze around doing nothing. Moreover, she didn't want to feel like she had to entertain a man to keep him from getting bored while she managed her businesses and wrote her cookbook.

"Does he like food?" Jane asked.

Leslie laughed. "I'm sure he does. Most men do."

Of course, men liked food. It was only women who fought to live up to society's expectations of what a woman should look like and eat.

"Is that all you have about him?" Jane asked.

"He's only interested in a long-term relationship...and children." Leslie hesitated, and then added, "The man is looking for a bride, but adds it has to be the right woman."

Jane's heart swelled. For the past seven years, she'd watched women her age and younger getting married and posting pictures of their husbands and babies on social media. Jane wanted all of that. The adoring husband, the swollen belly and the resulting chubby-cheeked babies.

She glanced down at her bikini-clad, thin body and sighed. She was ready to give up the perfect skin and body for all of that. She wanted to be a bride, but it had to be for the right man. Unless she put herself out there, she'd never meet him.

"Okay," Jane said. "What do we do next?"

Leslie laughed. "I give him your profile, and he decides from there whether he's interested enough to email you for a date."

Jane's heartbeat thudded against her eardrums. "What if he doesn't like my profile?"

"The program's algorithms matched you two. He's going to like what he hears. Let me get going on this. Hopefully, he'll contact you soon."

"Okay, thanks." Jane ended the call and set her phone down in a haze of panic.

The man sounded amazing. He liked what she liked, and he wanted what she wanted. They sounded like a match made in heaven. What could go wrong?

Everything.

Jane left her lounge chair and walked out into the afternoon sun. The Texas heat beat down on her exposed skin. She barely felt it she was so deep in her thoughts about her match.

She paced back and forth along the edge of the pool. No matter how much she paced, she couldn't slow her heartbeat, and she was getting hotter by the minute. With every nerve stimulated and her pulse racing, she had to do something to burn off the adrenaline generated by the mere thought of going on a date with a stranger.

The water beside her beckoned.

Jane dove into the pool and swam from one end to the other, up and back. After several laps, she got her breathing under control and her pulse moving to a more normal pace for someone swimming. When she rose out of the pool, she felt more in control.

Raising her face to the sun, she took a deep breath and squared her shoulders.

Dating was nothing to get into a panic about. Like any other business decision, she needed to approach it with logic and determination. If she wanted a family of her own, she had to pursue it with her eyes wide open and all the facts laid out before her.

She had to meet the man and get to know him to determine if he was going to be her husband and the father of her children.

No pressure. She could do this.

With that internal pep talk, she toweled dry and lifted her cellphone to calmly check her email.

She scrolled through her usually business-related missives from her agent, marketing firm and accountant and the usual spam. When she saw the email forwarded through BODS, she sank back onto the lounge chair, her heart racing and her legs shaking uncontrollably.

Was this it? Would it be from her match? Was he asking her out? She hesitated, her finger hovering over the link. Finally, she touched the email and it came up.

Hi, Jane, my name is Max.

Jane's heart skipped several beats. Max. His name was Max. It was a good name, strong and sexy. Butterflies kicked up in her belly and a slow burn coiled lower. Okay, so far so good. She took a deep breath and read on.

By now, you know BODS thinks we're a match. If you're like me, you'll withhold judgment until we've had a chance to meet in person and get to know more about each other.

Yes. He was right. They needed to meet. Profiles only told them so much about each other. Talking in person, seeing body language and facial expressions would tell much more than a list of likes and dislikes.

I'd like to take you to dinner, but not at the usual fancy restaurant.

Okay…. Jane's brow furrowed.

If you're up for adventure, I'll pick you up at six tomorrow evening. Wear jeans and close-toed shoes suitable for hiking. Hat and sunglasses are recommended. If you need character references that I'm not a serial killer, talk to Leslie. She knows me.

All I need from you is a yes or no and where to pick you up.

Jane sat back in her lounge chair.

Adventure? Jeans on a first date? Hiking? Her head spun as she scrolled through her recent calls and hit Leslie's number and put her on speaker. While it rang, Jane switched back to the email from Max and reread every word.

Leslie answered on the first ring. "Did he email you?"

"Yes," Jane responded, her voice too breathy for her liking.

"And?"

Jane shrugged. "I'm not sure what to think."

"You're killing me," Leslie cried. "What did he say?"

Jane stared at Max's words. "He wants to take me on an adventure?"

"Huh?"

"If I say yes, he'll pick me up at six tomorrow."

"And he said he was taking you on an adventure?"

Jane read the email out loud. "What do you think?"

Leslie laughed. "I think he's going to take you on a different kind of date."

"What do you know about...Max," Jane asked.

"I've vetted all my clients. As he said, he's not a serial killer. He's actually a good friend of a friend of mine. If my friend trusts him, I trust him."

"So, what do you think? Should I go?"

"Do you like adventure?"

"I don't know. It might depend on the kind of adventure."

"Do you like spontaneity?" Leslie probed.

"Sure," Jane said. "When I'm the one being spontaneous, and I know what I'm about to do."

Leslie laughed. "You said you were ready to start dating."

"I was wrong." She added in a softer tone, "Frankly, I'm scared."

"What do you have to be scared of?"

"That he won't like me for me." Jane sighed. "I'm

not just the model with the fancy hair and makeup. There's a real person beneath all that. I want to be loved for me, not the mask I put on every day."

"Then show him you," Leslie said. "Forget all the makeup. Wear your hair how you do on your days off. Wear the jeans he suggests—"

"Holy cow," Jane interrupted.

"What?"

"I'm not sure I own a pair of regular jeans."

Leslie laughed. "I'd offer you a pair of mine, but they'd be too short for your long legs. And I'm sure they'd be too big around the hips and waist."

"I'd give my eyeteeth for your figure," Jane said. "You're petite, curvy and beautiful."

Leslie snorted. "And you're tall, svelte and incredibly gorgeous. With or without makeup." She paused. "So, you're going to say yes, aren't you?"

Jane drew in a breath and let it out. "Yes."

Leslie's squeal erupted through the speaker.

Jane laughed. "You'd think you were the one going on this 'adventure date.'"

"What can I say?" Leslie chuckled. "I get excited when BODS brings people together."

"We're not together yet," Jane cautioned. "He might think I'm a dog when he sees me without makeup. And jeans do nothing for my figure."

"I'm sure he'll look past all that. He sounds like he only wants to get to know you. Not the clothes you wear."

"I don't know. I haven't played outside since I was a kid. What if I can't keep up with him on this adventure? I noted that I was in good shape, but that's all on my personal trainer. And all of that work is done in the gym."

"You'll be able to keep up. As my mother always said, *Don't borrow trouble.* Go with the flow and get to know the guy."

"Yes, Mom," Jane said, feeling only slightly better after talking with Leslie.

"Go. Answer his email and get to a shop to buy those jeans."

"Do you know how hard it is to buy jeans for a woman who's five-feet-eleven?"

"As hard as it is to find jeans to fit a curvy woman who's five-feet-two-inches tall?"

"Touché." Jane could only imagine being that tiny and precious and cute.

"I want all the details after your night out with Max," Leslie said.

"I'll let you know. Right now, I need to answer his email. He wrote so much. What should I say?"

"Yes!" Leslie answered. "And where he can pick you up."

"Ooo." Jane tapped her chin. "I don't want him to know everything about me, at least not yet. I used my real name instead of my modeling name on the profile. I don't want him to know I'm loaded."

"I'm sure he won't care," Leslie assured her. "You

could meet him in a neutral location like a coffee shop."

Jane nodded. "I know a coffee shop a mile away from my house."

"Perfect," Leslie said. "Good luck and have fun!"

After ending the call with Leslie, Jane pulled up the address of the coffee shop, then copied it and pasted it in her response to Max with the word *Yes.*

She didn't give herself time to second-guess her decision. Without hesitation, she pressed send.

The email blasted off into cyberspace, and she couldn't take it back.

How long would it take for him to read it? Would he respond?

Jane pushed to her feet, holding her cellphone out in front of her, willing an email to come through acknowledging hers.

She waited.

And waited.

A minute passed.

Then another.

"This is ridiculous," she murmured and set the cellphone on the table beside her lounge chair and turned her back on it, debating diving back into the pool for another eight laps.

She'd taken one step toward the edge of the pool when her cellphone chirped the sound indicating a new email had arrived.

Jane spun, grabbed for the phone and knocked it to the ground.

It slid beneath the lounge chair.

Jane dropped to her knees and reached for it, her heart racing and her breath coming in ragged gasps.

When she finally had the phone in her hand, she brought up the email application and stared at it.

Her laundry was ready for pickup at the local dry cleaners.

Her shoulders sank and she shook her head. "Am I really that desperate?"

The answer was yes.

She chuckled at the picture she must make...on her knees, clutching her cellphone like a magic wand that would transform her humdrum life into a fairytale.

Then her email application pinged again, and an email came up from the BODS exchange.

See you tomorrow at 6:00. Max.

CHAPTER 4

MAX DROVE around the block several times, not wanting to arrive at the coffee shop too early. He didn't want to appear too anxious to meet his *match.* And the jury was still out on whether or not this woman was his match.

He hoped he'd recognize her when he saw her. And he should. Not many women were five-feet-eleven. And she'd be wearing jeans if she'd gone along with his suggestion.

He pulled his truck into a parking space and dropped down out of the driver's seat. His pulse ratcheted up as he locked the truck.

It's just a date, he reminded himself.

But if this date went well, it could be his last first date for the rest of his life.

The pressure was on.

From the start, he'd approached this match as a

test the woman would have to pass. If she was the one he was destined to marry, it was kind of a...bride test. Would she pass? Would she be the woman he would promise to love, honor and cherish until death?

But as he'd driven to the designated location, he began to realize it was as much a test he'd have to pass from her point of view.

Would he be the kind of guy she'd want to love for the rest of her life? Would he pass *her* test?

At that point, he wasn't quite as sure as he had been about taking her on an adventure date. Not that it would be all that adventurous. He wasn't going to ask her to go rock climbing or hang gliding.

But he did want to make sure she was into the outdoors and liked nature and animals. After years playing football, and now, looking forward to spending much of his time outside on the ranch, he wanted someone to share his love of sunshine and nature.

As he pushed through the door of the coffee shop, he held his breath and prayed she had come and that she really was the woman he was dreaming of.

His gaze went to the first woman he saw, a petite brunette sitting with her laptop open, going through her social media as if her life hinged on it.

Not her.

Jane's profile said she was tall and blond.

His gaze moved on to the next booth. Someone with short blond hair sat with her back to the door.

Max started that way, his palms suddenly sweating. This was it. It had to be her.

He was just reaching out to tap her on the shoulder, when someone tapped him on his shoulder, stopping him in his tracks.

"Excuse me," a feminine voice said from behind him. "Are you Max?"

The person in the booth turned, revealing a young man with a blond mustache.

His cheeks burning, Max spun to face a tall, slender woman wearing sunglasses and a floppy hat. Her hair was pulled back behind her head. Since it was covered with the hat, he couldn't tell exactly what color it was. "Yes, I'm Max."

She held out her hand. "I'm Jane."

He took her hand in his. Her fingers were long and slender, and her skin was smooth and silky against the calluses on his palm.

A surprising shock of electricity touched his nerves and rippled up his arm into his chest.

She gave his hand a firm shake. Not too hard, not too soft, but firm.

He liked that he didn't have to look way down to see her face. Other than the tall drink of water Sean had fixed him up with, Max hadn't dated many tall women.

Trying not to be too obvious, he swept her with his gaze from tip to toe.

A little too thin, and her jeans looked too new, making him glad he'd dressed in one of his newer pairs. He'd almost opted for his favorite pair that he loved to work in, but they were stained and had a couple of holes worn through a knee and near his back pocket. Yeah, he'd have to throw them in the trash soon and break in another pair.

"Nice to meet you, Jane," he said.

"Nice to meet you, too," she said softly.

Her voice was melodic, not high-pitched or screechy.

So far, so good.

He wished she'd take off the sunglasses and hat so he could see more of her. But then, he'd recommended them, and it would appear too obvious if he asked her to remove them.

"Ready?" he said.

She nodded. "I think so. I wasn't sure what to expect in the way of an adventure."

"Don't worry, it won't be over the top. We're not going rock climbing. We're going to visit a ranch."

"A ranch?"

He nodded. "Ever been on one?"

She nodded. "Briefly."

"Then you know what to expect."

Her answering nod was slower.

"Do you ride?"

"Ride what?" she asked.

This was going to be harder than he'd thought.

"Horses."

"I don't know. I never have." She smiled, her pale lips spreading wide to display perfect white teeth. "But I'm willing to learn."

He nodded. She didn't ride horses. Max tried not to chalk up a mental strike against her, but he couldn't lie to himself. He'd hoped he'd find someone who loved riding horses as much as he did. At least, she was willing to learn.

"Your profile says you like animals."

"I do," she said.

"Good. Because there are a lot of animals on the ranch."

She nodded. "I look forward to seeing them."

He led the way out to his truck and opened the door for her.

She stepped on the running board and easily climbed up into seat, settling back into the contoured leather.

Max closed the door and rounded the hood to climb into the driver's seat. Nothing was more awkward than a first date, and he was feeling it. And based on how stiffly she sat beside him, she was feeling it, too.

With his hand on the start button, he paused. "Look, this doesn't have to be hard."

She turned toward him, her brow puckering. "What do you mean?"

"We don't know each other, but it doesn't have to be hard. We're just two adults going to visit a ranch. No expectations of anything other than getting out in the sunshine and breathing fresh air. I promise not to make any moves, and I don't expect anything from you, other than, I hope you'll enjoy the meal I had prepared." He held out his hand. "Deal?"

She nodded and placed her hand in his.

That same current of electricity zapped him and spread up his arm and throughout his body.

What the hell?

"Deal," she said with a smile. "I have to admit, I've never been on a blind date."

His lips twisted. "I have, back in college."

She shot him a glance. "Not good?"

"Let's just say, it wasn't a pleasant experience."

"I'm sorry to hear that." She turned to face the front windshield. "Couldn't have been easy to agree to another."

He touched the start button. "Leslie assured me her program was fool-proof."

Jane laughed nervously. "She did, didn't she?"

"I guess time will tell, right?" He glanced her way.

She bit down on her full, bottom lip. She wasn't wearing lipstick or any makeup for that matter…that he could see beneath the sunglasses.

He was really beginning to wish he hadn't suggested the hat and sunglasses and was beginning to hope for some clouds on this sunny afternoon. If all went according to his plan, they'd be out after sunset, and she'd have to take off those darned glasses. He wanted to see her eyes, the rest of her face and her hair.

Not that any of that mattered, he reminded himself. Hadn't he said looks weren't what he was most concerned about? Her mind and her personality were more important.

Still, the fact he couldn't tell what she looked like left a mystery about her that was frustrating him.

He forced himself to relax against the driver's seat and focus on the trip ahead.

"How far is the ranch?"

"It's about forty-five minutes out of town." He looked her way. "If that bothers you, we don't have to go."

She shook her head. "Not at all. Leslie's nothing, if not thorough. If she's vetted her clients, I trust her process." She turned toward him. "But if you're having second thoughts, we don't have to go."

He grinned. "No. I'm in." Max shifted into reverse, backed out of the parking space and shifted into drive. He left the office complex and drove out of Austin, heading northwest toward his ranch near Hellfire and Hole in the Wall.

He knew the road like the back of his hand. Once he left the traffic behind, he had no excuse for maintaining silence. He had to come up with small talk. God, he hated small talk. Why couldn't people just enjoy being with each other without having to come up with something to say.

"It's nice to be with someone who doesn't expect you to talk," Jane said.

He glanced toward her, expecting to see evidence of sarcasm.

But she was smiling softly, her face turned toward the road ahead.

"Agreed," he said. Well hell, what else was he supposed to say?

Ten miles passed. Then twenty. And he still didn't know any more about her than what was on her profile.

"I'm not much of a conversationalist," he offered.

"I'm enjoying the scenery. You don't have to entertain me. It's nice to be away from the hustle and bustle of big cities and relax in the countryside." She pushed her hat off her head and settled it into her lap. "I'm glad we're not going to a restaurant for our first date."

She had light blond hair, the color of corn silk. It was pulled back in some kind of braid that started at the crown of her head and hung down to the middle of her back between her shoulder blades.

Okay, so she was a blonde.

So was he.

Max had always pictured himself with a brunette.

Again, he had to remind himself looks didn't matter, as long as she wasn't fixated on looking different than her natural self.

From what he could see, she was pale, her skin appearing soft and smooth. He had sunscreen at the ranch house. She'd need it where they were going, until the sun set. He'd hate to be the cause of a massive sunburn, all because he wanted to take her out on the ranch and more or less test drive her ability to adapt to ranch life.

If she ended up being *the one*, he wasn't giving up his ranch to please her. This was his life after football. Crowds and cities were his past. He wanted a partner to share his love and passion for ranching and the outdoors.

She didn't ride horses, but her profile said she liked the outdoors.

"You don't ride horses, but do you ride a bicycle?"

"I haven't since I was really small." She grimaced. "Really, since training wheels. But I'm willing to learn again."

"Do you hike?"

"Not really."

"Play tennis?"

She shook her head.

"Golf?"

Jane bit down on her bottom lip. "No."

"What is it you like to do in the outdoors?" he

asked, at a loss for another sport she might be interested in."

"I like to swim in my—" She clamped her lips shut for a moment, and then started over. "I like to swim."

Based on her pale skin, she didn't swim outside much. "Do you have a pool near you?"

She nodded, looking out the passenger window, her face turned away from him, but reflecting in the glass. "Yes."

"How do you not burn?" he asked.

She turned a smile toward him. "I only swim at night. Otherwise, I'd burn to a crisp."

Max nodded. That would explain the lack of a tan. "What else do you like to do outdoors?"

"I like to walk. I love the scents of flowers and evergreen trees." She raised her eyebrows. "What about you? What do you like to do outside?"

He laughed. "Everything. Even sleeping beneath the stars on a cloudless night."

"Sounds glorious," she said on a sigh. "City lights keep people from seeing the stars."

"Have you always lived in a city?"

She shook her head. "When I was really young, we lived in a small town between Dallas and Waco. I remember the stars shining so brightly, and I could actually see the Milky Way. I've missed the stars."

Max stared up at the clear blue, Texas sky and smiled. "I think I can help you there."

She smiled his direction, her full lips stretching

across those pearly, white teeth. "Is the ranch out far enough away from the city?"

He winked and lifted his chin toward the open road and the wide-open spaces. "You tell me."

Jane clapped her hands. "I so look forward to the sun setting."

"And the sunsets out here are spectacular. But don't take my word for it. You can judge for yourself."

Jane leaned back in her seat, her smile softening, but still there, all the way to the stone and iron, arched gate announcing the entrance to the Live Oak Ranch.

"You work here?" she asked, leaning forward.

He owned it, but she didn't have to know that. Not yet. "I do. Me and some of my buddies spent the last couple of days hauling hay from those fields." He nodded to the freshly cut hay fields. "There are over three hundred head of cattle and ten horses on the ranch."

"Wow. That's a lot of animals," she said.

"That's just the horse and cattle. We have a variety of goats, chickens, pigs, dogs and cats. And that's the domestic animals."

"There's more?" she asked.

He nodded. "The ranch has over six hundred acres with abundant wildlife. We have turkey, quail, fox, coyote, and the occasional lynx and mountain lion pass through." His lips twisted. "And the usual raccoons, opossums, ringtails and armadillos, as well as a variety of snakes and lizards."

"Are you sure you don't work as a game outfitter, or something?"

"No, ma'am. When you work the land, you get to know all the critters and even the types of soil you have to grow things."

She raised her hands. "I believe you. Please tell me you're not going to introduce me to all of those today."

He wanted her to like animals, but had he come on too strong with his laundry list of what she'd find on the ranch? "Sorry, I didn't mean to get carried away."

She touched his arm. "You must love it out here."

"I do. It's important to me."

She nodded. "And if it's important to you, it needs to be important to whomever you share it with." Her smile bloomed again. "It sounds wonderful. I'm sure I'll love it, too." Her smile slipped. "Except for maybe the part about the snakes. I've only held a snake once for a photo sh—" She stopped in mid-sentence and bit down on her bottom lip before continuing. "It was a boa constrictor. I think it was hungry, because it tightened its hold on me while I had it draped around my neck." She gulped, her hand rising to her throat, her pale face growing paler.

"Seriously? How'd you get it off?"

"The snake handler waved a chicken in front of it. Apparently, chicken was its favorite food."

"Thank goodness," Max added. "Who would do that to a woman? Did you tell him that you didn't want to hold the snake?"

"It's okay. That was a long time ago."

He could tell it still affected her, by the way her hand remained resting against her neck. "Don't worry. I won't make you hold a snake. We do have a variety of them on the ranch. But I'll do my best to keep them away from you while you're here."

She gave him a tremulous smile. "Thank you."

"Other than snakes, do you have any issues with any other animals?"

"I don't think so," she said. "I haven't been around farm animals, so I can't tell you. I had a cat once. But that was when I was very young. She slept with me. I remember her having very soft fur." Her voice trailed off. "Sorry, I like animals, but I haven't been around many. I did pet a tiger once."

"A tiger?"

"Yes, and I stood next to a bear until he got cranky."

"You're a couple animals up on me. I can't say I've ever been close to either of them, other than at a zoo."

She shrugged. "I think as long as they're well-fed and happy, they're not hard to work with."

"Talk to the trainers who've been killed by their

pet lions, tigers and bears."

A shiver shook her frame in the seat beside his.

"Were you at some kind of petting zoo or safari?"

She shook her head. "No, the animals had handlers."

She didn't go into any more detail, and they'd arrived at the sprawling, two-story limestone and cedar ranch house with its wraparound porches on both levels and a huge barn to the west of the house.

"The house is beautiful," Jane said.

"It was built four years ago, so it has all the bells and whistles, from a pool out back to a theater room for watching the latest movies or football games."

"Impressive," Jane said. "The owner must have put a lot of thought into it."

So, she didn't think he was the owner, only the ranch hand who worked at the ranch. He didn't disavow her of that impression. Max thought it best she like him for being him before she realized he had enough money to build several mansions and buy even more acreage.

Rather than park in front of the house where he usually did, he drove around the back and pulled to a stop between the house and the barn.

He climbed down and rounded the front of the truck to open the door for Jane.

She eased onto the running board but missed getting enough of it to hold her. Her foot slipped off, and she fell forward into Max's arms.

He caught her easily, crushing her to his chest until she got her feet beneath her and could stand on her own.

Something about the way she felt in his arms made him feel odd. Sort of like déjà vu.

"Are you all right?" he asked, leaning back to look at her face. Those damned sunglasses. He couldn't read her expressions, because he couldn't see them.

She turned her face up to his and grimaced. "Sorry. I'm not usually so clumsy."

"No worries. Big trucks take some getting used to."

She nodded. "Thanks for catching me."

Again, that feeling of déjà vu struck him, but he couldn't put his finger on it. "As long as you're not hurt, we can move on to the next leg of our adventure."

Her eyebrows rose above the rims of the sunglasses. "You mean we're going farther?"

He nodded with a crooked smile. "We're not staying here. I have a special dinner planned in a special location."

She stepped out of his arms and tilted her head. "Are you sure you're not going to lead me off into the boondocks and make me find my way back?" She propped a hand on her hip. "This isn't some sort of test, is it? Like the Army dumping rangers in a swamp where they have to survive for a week eating snakes and bugs." She shivered. "I like animals all right, but I draw the line at eating bugs."

Max laughed out loud. "No. No. I'm not going to lose you in the swamp. We don't have a swamp on Live Oak Ranch. And I won't leave your side. Remember, I promised to keep the snakes at bay."

She nodded. "Still not convinced."

"I was going to take you on a horseback ride, but since you don't ride yet, we'll go on four-wheelers."

"Four-wheelers? Like ATVs?" she asked. "Would it help to know I haven't driven one of those any more than I've learned to ride a horse?" She shook her head. "I feel like I might be failing your test."

The slump of her shoulders made Max reach for her hands. "No. I don't want you to feel like you're failing anything. In fact, I already like your spunk. I'm impressed that you've actually petted a tiger. And I thought I was badass for having ridden a bull."

"You have?" Her fingers curled around his. "That sounds much more dangerous than my boa constrictor."

He rubbed the back of his neck. "It wasn't pleasant. I didn't stay on long. The bull convinced me that I didn't want to do the rodeo circuit." He'd been lucky he hadn't broken anything. Having been on the fast track for a football scholarship at Texas A&M, the bull riding fiasco could have cost him his education and his chances to play on an NFL team.

"Yeah, the rodeo wasn't my thing. It was a dare

from some of my high school friends," he admitted.

"Some friends."

He held out his arm. "If you're up for it, we'll move on. Your chariot awaits."

"Again, I've never driven an ATV."

"It's okay. They've made them pretty simple. All you have to do is shift it into forward and press your thumb on the accelerator."

"Thumb? Not foot?"

"That's for a car."

"Right," she said. "I knew that. But isn't a four-wheeler like a motorcycle?"

"It is."

"Don't you twist the handle?"

"Not on these. It's all in the thumb. The brakes are on the handle, and there's one by your foot. Come on. I'll show you. You'll be an expert before we leave the barnyard."

"Do you have clearance from the owner to use the ATVs?" she asked.

"I do. He's okay with me using anything on the ranch."

She glanced around. "Does he not live here?"

"Sometimes," he said, hating the white lies, but he wasn't ready to reveal who the owner was. Not yet.

He stopped short of the barn and turned to her. "Wait here."

"Okay."

He threw open one of the big doors on the barn

and strode inside. The barn smelled of fresh hay from the bales he and his friends had stacked in the loft the day before.

The horses he'd had moved to the stalls in preparation for an evening ride nickered.

"Sorry, no ride for you tonight," he called out. He ducked into the barn's office. Roy Tate sat in his office chair with his boots up on the desk, his hands working the leather strap of a girth. "Hey, bossman," he said. "Did your date stand you up?"

Max hurriedly closed the door. "Don't call me bossman. And no, she's waiting outside the barn."

Roy dropped his feet to the ground and rose from his chair. "I need to see this. You say a computer matched you two? Damn, if there's hope for you, you think there's hope for me?"

"Hell, no. You're too stuck in your ways." Max glanced over his shoulder. "Jane doesn't know I own this place. I'd like to keep it that way, for now."

Roy's brows rose up into the dark hair hanging over his forehead. "Seriously? How the hell you gonna impress her if you don't tell her?"

Max frowned. "That's just it. I want her to like me. Not my holdings."

Roy's eyes rounded. "Oh. Well that's a horse of a different color. Whatcha want me to do?"

"Nothing. We're taking the ATVs out to the lake. You can turn the horses out to pasture once we're out of the barnyard."

Roy gave him a mock salute. "Gotcha. And my lips are numb."

"Mum. Your lips are mum."

Roy frowned "Mine are numb. I don't know what yours are."

"Never mind." Max hurried to the refrigerator. "You didn't eat the meal I had Cookie prepare, did you?"

"No, but I wanted to. You put enough notes on it, I couldn't miss them." He cupped his crotch. "And I kinda like my parts where they are."

Max pulled out the basket he'd had his chef prepare with fried chicken, potato salad and beans. He'd had him throw in a bottle of wine and a couple of stainless-steel stemless goblets. To keep his foreman from raiding the food, he'd written ten notes and taped them to the basket threatening to cut off the foreman's balls if he so much as touched the food.

"Glad you can read," he said, a smile playing at the corners of his mouth.

"Can I help it I have a thing for Cookie's fried chicken?"

"I'm sure he has some left over for your dinner tonight. Just wait until we leave to go up to the house."

"Yes, boss—" He caught himself and finished with, "Moose."

"And don't call me Moose." Max shot another

glance over his shoulder. Thankfully, Jane hadn't followed him into the barn. "She doesn't know I played in the NFL."

"Well, hell," Roy exclaimed. "What does she know?"

"That I work on the ranch. Nothing more, nothing less."

Roy shook his head. "Think it's a good idea to start off with lies?"

"They're not exactly lies."

Roy gave Max a narrow-eyed glance. "If they aren't the truth, what are they?"

"I do work at the ranch," Max said, his cheeks heating. "That's the truth." It was, but it wasn't all of the truth and Max hated lying by omission.

Roy snorted. "Yeah, but not for pay."

"No kidding." Max tipped his head toward the loft. "If not for me and my friends, all that hay would still be sitting out in the field."

Roy held up his hands. "Hey, I'm not judging or complaining. Damned glad to get the help. And damned glad to have a job."

"Now, help me get the four-wheelers out of the back."

"Already done. They're waiting in a stall, gasoline all topped off." Roy pushed his thumbs through his belt loops and rocked back on his heels, a grin on his face. "Didn't think your date would be all too keen on riding a horse she hasn't been on. Especially on a first date."

"Worse than that, she's never been on a horse." Max still hadn't come to grips with that. But then, how many city women had even been close to a horse?

Why hadn't BODS found him a country girl? Wouldn't that have been a better fit?

He hurried to the stall Roy indicated and revved the engine on the first ATV. Today would be a make or break first date.

An image of Jane standing outside the barn in her new blue jeans and sunglasses flashed through his mind. What were the chances of her making it through the day without breaking a fingernail or getting dirty?

His lips spread across his face in a grin. Wasn't that what he wanted? A woman who didn't care if she got dirty? One who didn't care if she broke a fingernail?

Not that he'd go out of his way to make that happen, but four-wheeling on the ranch in and of itself was dirty. If she was following him, his vehicle would kick up dust in her face. She'd get dirty, all right. Some women would be appalled and angry. How she handled it would be revealing.

Max found himself hoping she'd be okay with it. Ranching life was dirty but rewarding. If she didn't see it that way, she wasn't the right woman for him.

CHAPTER 5

JANE STOOD OUTSIDE THE BARN, looking around, wishing she knew more about ranch life and wishing she'd had more time to break in the new blue jeans. Thankfully, they had spandex in them and stretched when she moved. But they looked so dark and blue compared to the softly-worn look of Max's jeans.

She shrugged and tried not to worry about the little things. The fact she'd be driving a four-wheeler by herself was something she wasn't all too sure about. She hoped it was as easy as he purported it to be. Otherwise, she'd fail that particular test on their first date.

She was beginning to feel as if this date was a kind of obstacle course. If she made it through, he might ask her for a second date.

The thought made her a little angry and a whole lot more determined to show him that she could hang with the best of the ranch girls. She hadn't known the world of modeling when she'd jumped in at a very young age. She'd made a career and a fortune from her hard work, intelligence and determination. Surely, she could ride a simple ATV without crashing.

She could hear the deep hum of male voices inside the barn, but not what the men were saying.

Just as she had decided to enter the barn, she heard a dog bark.

Her head jerked around to the corner of the barn where a large, gangly hound raced around the side of the building, chased by a beagle with brown, floppy ears.

The lead dog spotted her and charged directly toward her.

Not used to large dogs, Jane held her hands in front of her and backed up a step, and then another.

The dogs didn't slow, barreling toward her.

Jane didn't have time to think. She braced herself for impact.

The hound veered to the left as he passed in front of her, but not soon enough to avoid clipping her leg with his big body.

Jane let out a squeal. The force of impact sent Jane sprawling across the hardpacked dirt, knocking the sunglasses from her face. She landed hard on her side and lay still for a moment, wondering if she'd broken anything.

Before she could rise to a sitting position, the hound and the beagle doubled back and converged on her face, licking her cheeks and eyes.

"Hey, I'm okay. You don't have to lick me." Shoving the animals back for a moment, she managed to push to a sitting position and grabbed her sunglasses. She slipped them in place.

The dogs resumed their apologetic and slobbery kisses.

Jane looped her arm around the hound's neck. "Really, I'm fine."

The roar of an engine sounded in front of her, and Max drove what appeared to be a frighteningly large ATV out of the barn, stopping it in front of her. He leaped off and squatted beside her. "Jane? Holy cow. What happened?"

"I think I just received the barnyard welcome." She pushed the larger dog's face out of hers. The beagle leaped up and swiped a long, wet tongue across her chin.

"Down, Lulu." Max said in a stern tone, lifting the beagle off Jane's lap and setting her on the ground beside her. He pointed a finger at the dog. "Sit."

For a moment, the beagle sat, her tail making a dust fan in the dirt.

The hound renewed his kissing attack on Jane's face.

Jane laughed and shoved him away.

"Down, Blue," Max said and shoved the animal

away. He shook his head and pushed to his feet. "The only way to get them to back off is to get you back on your feet." Max extended a hand to her.

She placed hers in his, and he yanked her to her feet so quickly, she couldn't get her feet under her before she crashed into his chest.

His arms wrapped around her, and he held her until she was steady. And then a little longer. "Are you okay?" he said, his voice rich and resonant, causing shivers to ripple across her skin.

Blue bumped his nose against her thigh, and Lulu jumped up on her calf.

Max frowned down at the dogs. "What is wrong with you two? You're never this friendly with strangers." He gave her a crooked smile. "They must like you."

She rested her hands against his solid chest, her breath still caught in her throat. She didn't often meet men who were taller than her or as muscular as this one. He had broad shoulders that could carry any burden easily.

"I'm glad," she said, her thoughts muzzy. Was she glad the dogs liked her, or that Max's shoulders were broad? Perhaps both? She liked being pressed against this big guy. A little too much. A lot too soon. Jane pushed back until Max's arms fell to his sides.

He bent to scratch behind Blue's ears. "Blue is friendly with everyone. But Lulu..." Max shook his head and reached out to fondle the beagle's ears.

"Now, she has more discerning tastes. It usually takes her a couple of hours to warm up to anyone new." He stared up at Jane. "You must be a dog person."

She shrugged. "I've never had a dog as a pet, but I've always liked other people's dogs, and they seem to get along with me."

He nodded. "Good. I hope you'll forgive their manners. I never got around to teaching them any."

"Don't people hunt with hounds and beagles?" she asked. "Is that why you have them?"

He laughed. "Not Blue and Lulu. They'd be hopeless hunting. Most likely, they'd scare everything away within a mile." He straightened. "They're rescues from a local shelter."

A man who loved animals and rescued them from shelters...? Jane's heart warmed to Max.

He turned toward the four-wheeler he'd brought out of the barn. "Ready for your first lesson?"

She fought a grimace and nodded. "Let's do this."

"It really is easy." He led her over to the ATV and tipped his head toward the seat. "Hold onto the handle and hop on."

She gripped one of the handles and swung her leg over the seat. Once she was in place, she looked up at Max. "Now what?"

"You turn the key to the on position."

She did and frowned. "Nothing happened."

"Because you have to hit the start button." He

showed her where the button was. "But make sure you have your foot on the brake down by your foot."

After he showed her the foot brake, gear shift, the hand brakes, throttle and start switch, he stood back. "Ready?"

Jane wasn't ready at all. She forced a smile and nodded. "Ready."

"Start your engine."

She checked that the shift was in neutral, turned the key and pressed her foot on the brake. "This button?" she asked, her finger hovering over the starter.

He nodded.

"It won't jump when I hit it?" she asked.

"Not if you keep it in neutral and have your foot on the brake."

She checked again to see that she was still in neutral and pressed her foot hard on the brake. Then with a deep breath, she pressed the starter button.

The ATV's engine roared to life and rumbled beneath her. A smile spread across her face.

"Good. Now, all you have to do is push the shift into gear and give it some gas."

Jane released the handlebar and shifted into drive. The four-wheeler leaped forward. She squealed and almost threw herself off the vehicle. Before she could, Max jumped onto the back, reached around her and grabbed the handles and steered the vehicle away from the barn. The ATV didn't go more than two feet before it stopped.

Jane's pulse raced, and her hands shook. "What did I do wrong?"

"You have to keep your foot on the brake when you shift from Neutral to Drive. As long as you're not on a downhill slope, you won't go far unless you give it more gas."

She leaned against him, happy he'd jumped on and certain he'd saved her from plowing into the side of the barn. "I'm not sure I can do this," she said.

"You're doing fine," he assured her. "Now, take it around the barnyard." He let go of the handlebar. "Go on. You can do this."

She curled her fingers around the rubber grips and rested her thumb against the throttle lever. "Like this?" She was sure to keep her foot on the brake pedal.

"Remember, you can use the hand brakes as well."

She nodded and reached her hands around the metal levers. Then, slowly pressing her thumb to the throttle lever, she eased the ATV forward.

"That's right," Max said, his breath stirring the hair around her ear. "Give it a little more gas and make a circle around the yard."

She did, amazed at how easy it was to maneuver the gas, brakes and direction. By the time she'd circled and came to a jerky stop in front of the open barn door, she felt infinitely better. "That was fun."

"I'm glad you think so, because we'll need either this form of transportation or horses to get to where I want to take you."

Her eyes widened, and she sucked her bottom lip between her teeth. "I think I can handle this better than a horse at this point. At least the ATV doesn't have a mind of its own."

"Exactly." He slid off the back of the vehicle. "Think you can handle it by yourself?"

She nodded, although she would have preferred him riding on the back, in case she did something wrong.

"I'll be right back." He disappeared into the barn and returned a couple minutes later riding another ATV, just like the one he'd left her sitting on. He also carried two helmets. Pulling to a stop beside her, he dismounted and held out the helmet for her. "Safety first."

"Gladly," she said, and slipped the helmet over her head. Without makeup, she'd felt more exposed than she had in a very long time. Even more exposed than when she strutted the runway in bikini panties and a fancy bra.

Her face, sans makeup, was plain, almost boring. At least, that's how she saw herself. Now, it was probably covered in dog slobber and dust.

Oh, well. If he didn't like this Jane, they weren't meant to be. She'd keep looking for the man of her dreams. One who would accept her the way she was.

Her modeling days were coming to an end. Beauty faded. The man had to look past the outside shell to the person and the heart beneath. Otherwise, he'd be disillusioned, when beauty faded, and they grew old.

Max settled his helmet on his head and tightened the strap.

Jane tried but couldn't figure out the strap beneath her chin.

"Allow me." Max brushed aside her hands and quickly adjusted the strap snugly beneath her chin.

The entire time his knuckles rubbed against her skin, she held her breath, butterflies fluttering against the insides of her belly and heat coiling lower.

Having Max so near set a firestorm of feelings akin to fear that shot adrenaline through her system. But more than fear, she felt a kind of heady antic-ipation.

Jane told herself it was anticipation of riding a four-wheeler cross-country when she'd never done that before. But she was only kidding herself. The anticipation had more to do with the man she'd be following.

He intrigued her, and his rough, working-man's hands made her wonder what they'd feel like skim-ming across her naked body.

Max climbed onto his ATV and led the way to a gate. He opened it without getting off the vehicle and waited for her to maneuver her way through.

Concentrating on not crashing into the posts on either side, or running into Max's ATV, Jane made it through before she drew another breath.

Once Max had closed the gate behind them, he took off across a pasture, turning every so often to see whether she still followed.

She did manage to follow, though she was certain he slowed down just for her. She actually liked it better when he left a longer gap between them. When he was too close, he kicked up a cloud of dust. She was sure by the time they arrived at their destination her skin would be several shades darker, with layers of dust coating it.

The farther they went, the more comfortable she got with the brakes and the throttle. Her first challenge was descending into a shallow creek with water running through it.

Max sped up on his way down and threw up a giant wave of water before climbing the bank on the other side and coming to a stop. He grinned from the other side and waved her on.

Jane studied the banks and the water and decided, if Max could do it, she could, too.

Letting off the hand and foot brakes, she applied her thumb to the throttle and sent the ATV down the bank and into the creek. As she descended, her thumb eased off the throttle lever.

Water splashed up around her, soaking her from head to toe. She came to a stop in the middle of the creek before she remembered to give the ATV some gas. When she did, she gave it a little more than usual, causing it to leap forward, nearly leaving her behind.

She held on, struggling to remain seated and climb up the other bank to stop beside Max.

When she did, she looked back at the creek, and then to Max, and smiled. "That was amazing! Can we do it again?"

He laughed. "There's another creek to cross. And you'll get to do it again on our way back." Max took off again, moving a little faster.

Jane applied her thumb to the throttle lever and raced after him, feeling a little wild and free. Who knew she'd like riding four-wheelers and splashing through the water? Never had she been on a date quite like this.

Though she'd wondered at his choice of locations and activities, Jane was glad Max had decided to take her on an adventure. She couldn't think of any other date she'd liked better...so far. With the joy of being outdoors and riding with the wind in her face, she wondered what other surprises Max had in store for her. If he truly was putting her through a test, she hoped she would pass. She hadn't had this much fun in...well, ever!

CHAPTER 6

MAX HAD YET to catch a glimpse of Jane's eyes, but her smile rivaled the sunshine.

When she'd gone down into the creek bed and almost stalled out, he'd thought he would be pulling her out of the water when the ATV bogged down with water in the carburetor. But she'd quickly hit the accelerator and climbed out of the creek and up the bank with the biggest grin splitting her face.

Her smile was catching, and he found himself returning it. She was like a kid at her first Christmas, marveling at all the wonder and excitement.

She wasn't a model with every hair in place and makeup hiding her true appearance. Actually, what he could see of her face was covered in dust. But before it was covered in the fine powder from trail riding, it had been clean of all that stuff women liked to wear.

He'd found it refreshing. Now, if he could get her to take off those darned sunglasses, he'd like to see her eyes.

Would she have blue eyes to match that corn-silk hair? Or that reddish-brown, the color of cold root beer on a hot day? Maybe she had green eyes like the leaves in spring or like moss on a tree on a snowy winter day.

When they got to their picnic spot, he'd be sure to find a shade tree to spread the blanket beneath. Then he'd see those eyes.

What was the saying?

Eyes were the windows into a person's soul.

The thought of eyes reminded Max of the model he'd caught in Vegas. Those violet eyes had stuck with him even though he'd seen them only once.

He shook off the image of the sexy model lying in his arms and focused on his requirements for the woman he hoped to marry someday.

Jane might not be as outdoorsy as he'd prefer, but she was showing that she could be game to try new things, including four-wheeling in the hot Texas sun.

And she'd passed the Lulu test. Lulu had never been that friendly with any of the other women Max had brought to the ranch. Blue didn't know a stranger, so his opinion didn't count. But Lulu was usually hard to win over.

They passed through another small stream and

stopped to open and close another gate before heading through another field.

Max glanced over his shoulder at the woman on the ATV behind him. She wasn't smiling, but that was a good thing. With as much dust as was flying up behind him, she'd end up with a mouth full of mud if she dared open her mouth.

Thankfully, he was headed for the creek where he liked to swim in the nude on a hot summer day. They could wash hands and faces in the clear, clean water before they settled down for the fried chicken Cookie had provided in the picnic basket.

At the top of the next hill, he slowed to a halt and waited for Jane to catch up.

She pulled to a jerky stop beside him. When she glanced down at the valley and the stream below, the grin returned. "Are we going through another creek?"

He shook his head. "No, that's where we're having lunch." His gaze swept the green, grassy valley. Trees lined a creek snaking through the middle. Water reflected sunlight through the gaps in the trees.

"It's beautiful," she said, her voice soft.

"It's one of my favorite places to come when I need time away from everyone and everything. Or when I want to take a dip to cool off after working in the heat."

"Sounds amazing." She shot a glance his way.

He nodded and gave his ATV a burst of fuel, sending it down into the valley. He led her to a quiet copse of trees overhanging a grassy glen beside a wide pool formed in the rocks by the creek.

Max stopped his four-wheeler, shifted into neutral and switched off the engine. He removed his helmet and set it in the front basket before getting off the ATV.

Jane pulled to a stop beside him and shifted into neutral.

He showed her how to lock the brake and then turn the key to kill the engine. Max unbuckled the strap beneath her chin. Jane slid the helmet off her head and laid it on the fuel tank. "That was fun," she said, pushing her hand through her tangled hair.

"I'm glad you liked it."

When she slid off the seat, her knees buckled.

He caught her against him and held her steady.

She laughed. "My legs feel like jelly."

"Like riding a horse for any distance," he said, "it takes some getting used to."

"I'll remember that." She straightened and looked around. "This is lovely."

"I think so."

She walked toward the water and bent to scoop up a handful. "Do you bring all of your dates on picnics here?" She removed the glasses and splashed the water on her face, making muddy trails down her cheeks. "Some impression I'm making. I think I have enough dirt on my face to make a mud pie." She set her sunglasses on the ground beside her and dug both hands into the water to splash it up into her face several times, washing away all of the dust from the ride. When she was finished with her face, she scrubbed her arms and hands, then shook off the water.

While she washed up, Max lifted the lid of the basket and pulled out a checkered tablecloth, which he spread on the ground. He anchored one corner with the basket to keep the wind from making off with the fabric.

Cookie had gone above and beyond his expectations. The chicken was wrapped in plastic bags. When he opened the bag, the scent filled the air and made his stomach rumble loudly.

Jane chuckled. "Hungry?"

"My chef—friend makes the most amazing fried chicken, potato salad and baked beans. I hope you're hungry."

"It sounds wonderful." She sat on the corner of the blanket, her sunglasses back on her nose. "What can I do to help?"

"You can help yourself to the food provided. Sorry, all we have is paper plates and plastic utensils."

She laughed, that smile lighting her face beneath the impenetrable sunglasses. "What's a picnic without paper plates and plastic utensils?"

"Right?" He returned her smile. "I brought a bottle of wine. I hope you like red."

"I like my wine dry," she said. "So, red is wonderful."

When he'd first met Jane, he found himself mentally tagging her with the old moniker "Plain Jane". However, now that he'd witnessed her smile, he didn't think of her as plain at all. He liked her smile.

He poured two stemless goblets of wine and handed one to her. He lifted his and held it toward her. "To new friendships."

"To friendship." She touched her goblet to his, and then sipped at the wine.

Jane chose a chicken breast from the bag and scooped a small spoonful of potato salad and baked beans onto her plate.

She ate all the large chicken breast before moving on to the potato salad. "The chicken was so good," she said, licking her fingers.

"I'm partial to the potato salad. I'm sure I'm biased, but I think it's the best of any I've ever had."

She speared a chunk of potato and brought it to her lips. As she deposited it onto her tongue, she leaned back her head and drew in a deep breath, her breasts rising beneath her shirt. Then she moaned, "Mmm."

Max's groin tightened.

Jane's reaction to the potato salad was as erotic as any porn movie, only better. It made him want to feed her the next bite to watch her do that again.

After chewing slowly and swallowing, she

straightened and smiled. "That's really tasty. Do you think he would give me his recipe?"

"I'll ask." He bit into his potato salad, half-expecting a similar orgasmic reaction. It was good, but her reaction was better. "Your profile stated that you're a cook…?"

"Actually, I'm between careers. I want to be a cook and write my own cookbook."

"Do you have any experience at being a cook?" he asked, biting into a forkful of baked beans.

"No," she said. "But I want to learn. I've signed up for a French cooking class in Austin next month. I can't wait."

"What was your previous career?" he asked.

She popped a spoonful of baked beans into her mouth and chewed. "Wow, the beans are almost as good as the potatoes." She scooped more beans onto her spoon and answered, "Fashion merchandizing." Then she popped more beans into her mouth and chased it with the wine. After she swallowed, she faced him.

"Have you always been a rancher?" she asked.

He hesitated, not wanting to go into his past profession. From what he could tell, she didn't know who he was.

Nonetheless, he'd practiced his answer to her question. "Not always."

"Oh, yeah?" She tilted her head to one side. "What did you do before ranching?"

He drew in a deep breath and told half the truth, "I was into sports management." And he had been... managing himself.

Her head tipped up and then down, as if she were taking him in from head to toe. "I can see that. You look like an athlete."

He smiled. "And what does an athlete look like?"

"All muscle and not a spare ounce of flesh," she answered.

He treated her to the same perusal, skimming her with his gaze. "I could say the same for you. All muscle, not a spare ounce of flesh."

Her lips pressed together, and she turned her head away. "I didn't get it from playing sports."

"No?" He tipped his head. "I could see you as a runner." She was thin and toned.

"I do cardio on a treadmill and elliptical. And when no one's watching, I like to dance, but just for exercise. I'm not very good at it."

"Have you ever done the two-step?" he asked.

She shook her head. "I haven't had any dance lessons."

"You don't have to have dance lessons to do the two-step." He covered the potato salad, beans and the packed them away with the remaining chicken into the picnic basket.

Jane gathered the plates and plastic utensils and stashed them in the plastic bag they'd arrived in.

Max shoved them into the basket with the food, pushed to his feet and held out his hand.

"Are we going?"

"No. You're going to learn how to two-step."

"Here?" she said, her head turning right then left.

He wanted to know what she felt like in his arms, although he was almost positive she'd feel good. By teaching her to two-step, he'd have a chance of holding her, without making her uncomfortable.

He looked around, his eyes narrowing, and then he winked. "No one's watching."

Her smile hit him in the gut. So far, he liked what he saw, but there was so much more to a relationship than looks. Sean had been right. Chemistry was important. He had to know there was chemistry between himself and Jane.

JANE PLACED her hand in his, sending a shock of awareness up her arm.

Max drew her to her feet, placed one hand at the small of her back, draped her hand on his shoulder, and held the other hand in his. "Just follow my lead."

"But there's no music," she protested, although weakly.

"We'll make our own." He held her firmly in his grip. "It's easy. Two quick steps and two slow steps. Start on your right foot moving backward. Ready?"

She shook her head. "No."

"Two quick, two slow, just like walking." He smiled. "I'll go really slow. Move your right foot first. Quick, quick, slooow, slooow."

She moved her right foot, matching the rhythm of his words. With his hand braced against her back, he led her in a wide circle.

Moving with Max felt as natural as breathing. Soon, they were dancing around the glen to the sound of his *quick, quick, slooow, slooow.*

Just when she thought she had the steps down, he stopped.

"Easy, right?" he asked.

She nodded. "But that's without music." Would music confuse her?

"Then let's put the steps to music." He gave her a twisted grin. "I can't hold a tune in a bucket, but I'll give it my best shot with a song my mother used to sing to me."

He led her a couple rounds of two-stepping to his words *quick quick, slooow slooow,* before he started to sing, "You are my sunshine, my only sunshine..."

Her heart swelled at the nostalgic tune. Her mother had sung that song to her as well. It brought back sweet memories she'd thought long forgotten.

Jane kept pace, her feet moving to the same beat as his, even when he wasn't saying *quick, quick, slow, slow.*

"You make me happy when skies are gray," he sang in a deep tone, his breath warm on her temple.

Jane closed her eyes and floated to the tune and the beat, her feet moving as if they had always known the steps, her hand warm and secure in his.

"You never know dear, how much I love you," Max's voice sang, the words growing softer, fading to a whisper.

Jane's gut clenched. Behind the safety of her mirrored sunglasses, she stared up into his face.

He was looking down at her, his gaze on her lips.

Jane leaned into him and lifted her chin. At that moment, she wished he'd close the distance between her mouth and his with a kiss as soft as his words.

"Please don't take my sunshine away." Max slowed to a stop on the last word and continued to stare down at her.

Then he reached up and tilted her chin. His hand moved to the sunglasses, pulling them from her face.

Jane blinked at the bright daylight, and then focused on the man still holding her in his arms.

His eyes widened for a moment, and then narrowed. "Do you believe in déjà vu?"

"I've never really thought about it," she said, her voice shaky.

"I can swear I've seen you before. But I haven't, have I?"

She'd had that feeling as well but couldn't quite put her finger on it. Jane shook her head. "I don't think so."

"It's the eyes. You have the same color eyes as someone I met not long ago."

Her cheeks heated at the intensity of his stare. "My mother said they were the same color as periwinkles."

He smiled down at her. "I would have called the color violet."

She nodded. "On my driver's license, they're listed as blue."

Max brushed his thumb over her temple and shook his head. "That's wrong. Your eyes are violet, not blue. And they're beautiful."

Her cheeks burned under his compliment. She'd been called beautiful for most of her life. Standing in front of Max, wearing blue jeans and no makeup, she felt more beautiful than she'd ever felt in her life.

For a model who'd had her image plastered over every major magazine at one point or another in her life, hearing Max call her eyes beautiful meant so much more.

Then his head descended, and his lips grazed hers in a feather-light kiss.

She swallowed the moan sliding up her throat, lifted up on her toes and engaged his mouth in a more substantial kiss, opening to him.

His tongue swept in to claim hers, caressing the length in a slow, sensuous glide.

Jane clung to Max, her fingers curling into the fabric of his shirt.

If Max let go of her at that moment, she wasn't sure her legs would hold her.

When he finally lifted his head, he stared down into her face. "I'd say I'm sorry for moving too quickly...but I'm not sorry."

She shook her head. "I'm not sorry either.

The corner of the picnic blanket lifted and wrapped around their ankles, distracting them from the intensity of the kiss.

Jane backed away, bending over to untangle her legs from the blanket. Her heart raced, and her mouth tingled from the pressure of his.

Wow...just wow. To keep from making eye contact with him, and revealing how much that kiss had meant, Jane gathered the blanket. Taking her time, she matched the corners and folded the blanket into a neat square that fit easily into the other side of the saddlebag.

Max lifted the basket and placed it on the front rack of his four-wheeler, strapping it down with bungee cords.

Finally, he turned to her.

Jane forced herself to look at him without the sunglasses hiding her eyes.

"Ready?" he asked.

She nodded. Ready for more than a trip back to the barn. Ready for this date to continue for much longer.

Alas, the sun was setting, and the shadows had lengthened and merged.

He waited for her to settle her helmet on her head and mount her ATV. Then he helped her get it started. Once she was ready, he slipped on his helmet and climbed aboard his vehicle.

Soon, they were racing across the fields, headed back the way they'd come.

Jane wondered if Max had felt the deep connection she'd felt with that kiss.

Or had the kiss disappointed him?

Jane's heart skipped several beats, and she let off the pressure on the throttle, falling behind Max on the lead vehicle.

She squared her shoulders and gave the ATV a shot of fuel, sending it shooting forward.

She couldn't worry about things out of her control. The best she could hope for was that he would ask her out again.

If he didn't... *She* just might have to ask *him*.

Jane pushed that thought to the very back of her mind, refusing to linger in such negativity or radical thinking.

CHAPTER 7

MAX COULD HAVE KICKED himself from here to tomorrow. What had he been thinking by stealing a kiss so soon on their first date?

Jane was special. Deep down, he already knew that. He couldn't jump her bones on their very first outing. But he had kissed her so long and deep, it might as well have been sex. She'd know that was exactly what he wanted.

Hell, he had a hard-on she couldn't have missed, pressed into her belly throughout that incredible, mind-blowing kiss.

He had to be more logical about this dating thing. Lust and emotions couldn't get in the way of making a rational decision. Logic was key to a lasting relationship. Lust didn't always last.

Oh, but it had flared like a mother-fu—

Logic. Think logic.

If he evaluated Jane's pros and cons, he might come up with a more analytical approach to the woman following him.

Con: she'd never ridden a horse.

Then again, she'd never ridden a four-wheeler, and yet she was keeping up with him as he raced across the pasture toward the barn. The woman was game.

Con: she didn't know much about ranching.

Then again, how many women had he known would have the first clue about anything to do with ranching? Not many.

Pro: she'd learned how to two-step and felt so good in his arms. Dancing and riding four-wheelers demonstrated her potential to adapt to new challenges.

It was a start, but was it enough? Ranching could be hard work. Then again, he had enough money to pay someone to do the hard work. How much did he expect his woman to do when it came to ranching?

He expected her to want to know what it entailed and, maybe, pitch in if they needed an extra hand.

Max's brow furrowed. Jane's hands had been soft and uncalloused. He couldn't picture her grabbing a bale of hay and throwing it onto a stack. Hell, he couldn't picture her getting dirt under her fingernails. Then again, she'd ridden behind him all the way, accumulating a thick layer of dust on her face and hadn't complained about it messing up her hair or makeup. That counted for something.

Pro: she had the most amazing violet eyes.

Nope. He couldn't think of any con to balance that one. Max felt as though he could fall into her gaze and never come out. Or ever want to come out.

Everything was moving too fast for him to get his arms around the entire experience. He wanted to skip past getting to know her on an intellectual level and go straight to the physical level.

He shook his head and gunned the accelerator, sending his ATV down the bank of the creek a little faster than he should have and at an angle that missed the shallowest spot. When he hit the deep water, the ATV skimmed halfway through it, and then sank like a rock, with him on it.

The water was only four feet deep, but the vehicle completely submerged, choking the life out of the engine.

Max swore and floated off the seat, struggling to get his feet beneath him.

Behind him, he heard the trailing ATV come to a halt at the top of the bank.

Before he could turn and yell for Jane to stay where she was, she'd cut off the engine, leaped out of her seat and scrambled down the steep bank, her feet sliding out from under her on the loose gravel.

Max couldn't get to her before her feet hit the slick mud his four-wheeler had churned up.

She screeched to a stop, her heels digging into the muck. When she pushed to stand, the mud caved in. Jane scrambled, her feet moving but gaining no purchase. Leaning forward like a snow boarder, she put out her arms and skied down the hill then flipped face first into the mud.

Max had waded toward her but hadn't reached her until she'd made her climatic landing.

He reached down and grabbed her arms, lifting her out of the mud. He held her while she planted her feet on the smooth pebbles of the creek bed. Water rushed around their knees.

"Are you all right?" he asked, smoothing some of the mud from her face. His thumb created a pale trail across her cheek. She couldn't have been muddier if she'd tried.

Her violet eyes shone out of the muddy mess. Then her lips spread, and a crooked smile parted the dark mud. "I'm getting you all muddy." She moved her hands where she'd braced herself on his chest. Two large prints remained, along with a smear where he'd crushed her body against his to help her balance.

He chuckled. "A little dirt never hurt anyone, as long as you're not hurt from that spectacular slide down the bank."

She shook her head. "The only thing hurt was my pride." Jane turned her head and spit mud out of her mouth. "Sorry."

"Don't be." He wrapped his arm around the small

of her back and led her deeper into the rushing creek water that came up to their knees. "Let's get some of this off you. How do you want to do this?"

She lifted her hands palms upward and grinned. "The only way I know how." Then she stepped back and laid down in the creek, submerging her head and letting water rush over her hair, face and entire body.

Max laughed and sat in the creek beside her.

Jane came up, rubbing her hands over her face to clear the remaining mud from the crevices around her nose, ears and eyelids. "And to think, women pay for mudpacks when they could come here and get them for free." She grinned at him.

Max stared at her.

With her hair slicked back from her face, he could see her high cheekbones and the beautiful arch of her eyebrows. Her full, sensuous lips were a pale pink, wet and very kissable. Her violet eyes twinkled with humor.

That déjà vu feeling washed over him again. The only other woman he'd known to have violet eyes was the model in Vegas.

His eyes narrowed. Jane could have been the paler, less stunning sister of that woman, if he went purely by the color of her eyes. But the model had worn thick makeup around her eyes and a dark lip color. Her hair had been slicked back, much like Jane's now, but they couldn't be the same woman.

Jane was makeup-free and almost wholesome in

the paleness of her skin and the way she wore her blue jeans.

And she was frowning at him.

"What?" she asked, swiping at her face. "Did I miss a spot?"

He shook himself out of the trance. "No. You got the majority of it. A shower will get the rest." He glanced toward his submerged ATV. "If you're okay, I'd like to pull my ride out of the water before we head back to the barn."

"What can I do to help?" she asked.

God, he liked her. What female would fall down a bank, bury herself in mud and still ask what she could do to help?

He pushed to his feet and held out a hand.

Jane took it and let him draw her drenched body out of the water. Her shirt lay plastered to her skin, the outline of a pink bra showing through the thin material.

Max didn't say anything, reluctant to make her even more self-conscious. But his body responded to the fact she wore a sexy bra beneath the plain shirt.

"The winch will do most of the work." He held her hand a moment longer. "Are you good standing on your own?"

She nodded. "I can do that."

He waded through the stream and carefully climbed the muddy bank to Jane's ATV. Then he drove it across the creek to the other side, paying attention to where the creek bed was shallower. He made it safely to the other side, where he parked the ATV and set the parking brake. "I'll need you up here when I pull my four-wheeler out of the water." He hurried back down to the stream and ushered Jane up the other side, careful not to let her slip back down into the water.

When she was safely on the other side, he grabbed the metal hook on the winch and slid back down the bank, pulling as much cable he could behind him. When he reached his ATV, he placed the hook securely on the chassis of the vehicle, shifted it into neutral and released the parking brake.

Then he hurried back up the bank and straddled the four-wheeler. "Hopefully, with both of us on the ATV, it will be enough weight to keep it from sliding down into the creek with the other one." He patted the seat behind him.

Jane's brow furrowed as she slid onto the seat behind him. "Are you sure this is going to work?"

"I promise, if it looks like it won't do the trick, I'll leave it and come back later to haul it out of the water with a pickup truck. Hold on and think heavy thoughts." He winked at her, and then turned the switch to power the winch. The little motor started turning, reeling in the cable until it was taut. The ATV beneath them jerked as the cable tugged on the one in the water.

Max revved the ATV's engine and shifted into

reverse. Between the wench and the reverse motion of the ATV, they budged the other vehicle in the water, dragging it through the deepest current to the bottom of the bank. The water helped to float it to that point, but the angle of the bank made it more difficult to drag it without the assistance of water floating the tires.

"Hold on," Max said. The little winch engine wouldn't be able to do all the work. He had to drag it out using the strength of the other ATV. He eased his thumb onto the throttle, edging the ATV backward a little at a time.

Jane wrapped her arms tightly around his waist and pressed her face against his back.

He hadn't planned on scaring her, but he hated leaving the ATV in the water. It would require a lot of work as it was having had the engine swamped.

An inch at a time, he moved backward. Several times, the tires slipped in loose gravel. They lost a couple of inches. Then the tires would engage again, and they'd continue backward.

Finally, the submerged four-wheeler crested the bank and came to a stop on level ground.

"We did it!" Jane laughed. "I thought for sure we'd end up down there with the other one." She climbed off the back and stood to the side, her hands clasped together, light dancing in her eyes.

Max shook his head and set the parking brake but

left the engine running before he turned to her. "I'm hurt that you didn't think we could do it."

"After sliding down the other side, I didn't think the ground would hold up." She grinned. "But you did it."

"I couldn't have done it without you. That little bit of extra weight helped." He unhooked the winch from the other vehicle and tried to start its engine. When he pressed the starter switch, the engine didn't even turn over.

"Guess we're riding double back to the barn." Max pushed the dead ATV away from the edge of the creek and parked it beneath a tree. After setting the parking brake, he turned to Jane and waved his hand toward her vehicle. "Hop on."

Her eyes narrowed. "Don't you want to drive?"

"I can drive anytime. This is your day of adventure."

She climbed onto the front and scooted forward, leaving room for him.

"Besides," he added. "I was the reckless one who drowned his ride. You had more sense than to get in over your ATV's head." He slid on behind her and wrapped his arms around her waist. "Go easy on me. I'm completely at your mercy."

She laughed and shifted into drive, released the parking brake and gave the ATV some gas. They took off so fast, she almost left him behind.

If he hadn't been holding on so tightly around her middle, he'd have been sitting in the dust.

At least that was his excuse for being as close as he was. The fact he could still see the pretty pink bra beneath her shirt had nothing to do with his desire to be close.

Uh-huh. Yeah, right.

JANE COULD BARELY BREATHE ALL the way back to the barn. Not because Max was holding her so tightly that she couldn't get air into her lungs. She couldn't breathe because she couldn't catch her breath.

With Max's arms wrapped around her middle and brushing against her breasts with each bump encountered, she couldn't think or remember to breathe.

One kiss and playing in the water fully clothed with the man shouldn't have her body on fire with desire, should it?

No.

But it did.

By the time they reached the barnyard and Max got off the back to open the gate, Jane was practically light-headed. The sun had set, and the gray light of dusk had deepened. The stars were just starting to appear.

She brought the ATV to a halt in front of the barn and climbed off, her legs wobbly from the long ride.

Max took the ATV from there and pushed it into the barn. A minute later, he emerged, hooked her elbow and guided her toward the house.

"Is this the end of our date?" she asked as they crossed the yard toward the porch.

"I promised you some stars. If you're still up for it..." He paused at the bottom of the porch steps.

She glanced down at her damp clothing. Not feeling at all pretty. How could he like her, if she looked like a drowned rat? "I'm not sure I'll enjoy them all wet." She gave him a lopsided grin. "Though it was fun getting wet."

Max chuckled. "Fun? You call sliding down a hill and landing face-first in the mud fun?"

She shrugged. "It was an adventure. And a little mud never hurt anyone."

"I think I can find you some dry clothes, and you're welcome to use the shower." He started up the steps, his hand still beneath her elbow.

She balked, staring up at the house. "Won't the owner care that you're using his house?"

"I live here," he said. "I can come and go as I please. And I can invite guests in as well."

"Are you some kind of groundskeeper for when the owner is away?" she asked.

"Something like that," he said, without meeting her gaze. "You can have the downstairs shower. I'll take the upstairs."

She followed him up the porch steps, stopping before the door to remove her water-logged shoes.

Max toed off his boots and held the door for her.

On the outside, the house was a pretty white limestone with cedar accents and a broad, wrap-around porch on both stories.

Inside the house, the floors were a dark wood, the walls a light off-white. He led her through a mudroom into a brightly-lit, spacious kitchen a chef would give his first born to work in. A six-burner gas stove had center stage against one wall with a pot filler spigot to make it easy to make a vat of stew. A farmhouse copper sink graced a huge center island, and speckled granite countertops were in abundance for food preparation activities.

"Wow," Jane said. "This kitchen is amazing." She studied every detail, wondering if she could transform her own into such a usable and happy place. She doubted it. Though her kitchen was large, it wasn't as big as the one before her.

"Coming from a cook, I'll take that as a compliment." He continued through the kitchen that opened up into a massive living room with floor-to-ceiling windows stretching across two of the long walls. The ceiling rose two stories high, giving the space a cavernous feeling that was open and welcoming.

They continued through the house to a bedroom with an adjoining bathroom.

"I'll find something dry for you to wear. We can

put your clothes in the wash. Hopefully, they'll be dry by the time we head back to Austin."

"You don't have to go to all this trouble. If we wait for my clothes to dry, it will be really late by the time we head back to Austin."

"I'd offer to let you stay the night, but I don't want to get my face slapped for moving too fast." He rubbed the side of his dirty chin. "Really, I don't mind taking you back tonight. I'm used to the drive, and I have a friend in Austin I can stay the night with."

Her heart had skipped several beats at the thought of staying the night in the same house with Max. Could she trust herself to sleep in separate beds, in separate rooms?

Not a chance.

The man had her tied in sensual knots.

She cupped his chin where his hand had been a moment before. "I'm not the violent type. I wouldn't slap you for suggesting I stay the night. But, if you don't mind, I'd like to be home before midnight." It took a lot of willpower to say those words, but she was proud of herself for doing it. She didn't want to appear to be too clingy or loose. For the love of Pete, they were still on their first date.

"I can make that happen." He jerked his chin toward the bathroom. "You can get started in the shower. There should be towels in the cabinet behind the door. I'll leave clothes here in the bedroom for when you get out."

"Thank you," she said and entered the bathroom, closing the door behind her. At that point, she leaned against the panel, closed her eyes and let go of the breath she felt like she'd been holding since they'd first met.

How could Leslie's program have chosen such a man? He was too perfect. He was hardworking, outdoorsy, seemed honest, and he wasn't a celebrity or bigshot in sports. He didn't care to go to the fanciest restaurant, nor did he expect her to dress to the nines and be made up perfectly at all times in case a reporter happened to show up and snap a picture.

With a smile on her face, she stripped out of her clothes and passed in front of the mirror.

Holy cow! She was a complete wreck. Her face still had smears of dirt and mud, and her hair was caked in mud.

She was surprised the man hadn't run screaming or thrown her in the back of his truck and hauled her back to Austin without showing her those stars.

Switching on the shower, she adjusted the temperature and stepped beneath the spray. Making use of the available bodywash and shampoo, she made quick work of cleaning every inch of her body of the offending dirt, washing the mud down the drain.

When she was finished, she dried her body and squeezed the moisture out of her hair. She found a comb in the drawer and worked the tangles out of her hair.

Wrapping the towel around her, she eased open the door, half-hoping she'd catch Max placing clothing on the bed.

The room was empty, but a neat stack of clothes lay on the bed and the door to the bedroom was closed.

So much for tempting the man by strutting out of the bathroom in nothing but a towel.

Chastising herself for being too eager, Jane crossed to the pile of clothing. He'd left an extra-large red, T-shirt with the Texas A&M logo imprinted on the front and a pair of gym shorts.

A shiver of desire rippled across her and pooled low in her belly. She'd be wearing his T-shirt and shorts without any undergarments beneath them. That would be as close to naked as she'd get to him on their first date. The thought made her feel absolutely decadent.

She smiled as she pulled the T-shirt over her head and the shorts up over her hips.

She adjusted the drawstring inside the shorts to keep them from sliding off. Then she knotted the hem of the T-shirt to one side to keep it from falling down around her knees.

Though her breasts hung free beneath the shirt, it was large enough to hide the fact that her nipples were taut and hard.

A quick glance in the bathroom mirror reminded her that she wasn't all that sexy with her hair damp and her face scrubbed clean. She looked more like someone's kid sister in her oversized clothes.

Good.

Maybe the kid sister reminder would keep her from throwing herself into Max's arms, begging him to take her to bed and make mad, passionate love to her.

Pasting a sisterly smile on her face, she exited the bedroom and wandered out into the living room.

Noise from the kitchen made her follow the sound.

She found Max pouring tea into iced glasses.

"I hope you like iced tea," he said.

"Unsweet?"

He nodded. "You can sweeten to taste. I prefer mine without sugar."

"Me, too."

"I like other forms of sweets." He reached into the refrigerator and pulled out a tray of cut-up fruit.

Jane smiled. "I much prefer natural sweets than cakes or donuts."

"Agreed. But I am a sucker for pies."

Jane drew in a deep breath and let it out on a sigh. "Apple pie with vanilla ice cream."

"My mother made the best sweet potato pie."

"I've never had sweet potato pie."

"It's like pumpkin, only better. I'll make one for you sometime."

The fact he wanted to make her a pie, gave Jane hope that they had a future beyond that night. But she didn't want to push him to nail down their next date.

They grazed on the fruit for a few minutes, standing at the granite counter, eating and not talking.

And it was a good thing. Jane couldn't think of anything to say other than she wanted to eat strawberries off Max's naked skin. No, saying something like that was far too soon in their relationship.

He was a rancher. A man who loved the simple life. How appalled would he be if she came on too strong too soon?

"We can take this outside," he offered.

She polished off another bite of cantaloupe. "I don't need any more. It was delicious. Thank you."

He stored the tray in the refrigerator and grabbed his glass of tea. "You can have something stronger, if you like. I'm staying with the tea since I'm driving later."

"Tea is wonderful." Jane wrapped her fingers around the cool glass and followed Max out a side door onto the porch.

He didn't stop at the porch but walked down to a patio area and a pool with a soft blue light glowing in the darkness.

"We'll watch the stars from here." He set his glass on a table next to a couple of lounge chairs. "You choose which one you'd like."

Jane settled into the one on the right and set her glass on a table on the other side of her chair.

Max walked over to what appeared to be a pump shed and flipped a switch. The lights in the pool blinked out. He returned to Jane's side, dropped into the empty lounge and stretched out his legs, crossing his arms behind his head. "I understand there's to be a meteor shower over the next couple of nights."

Jane stared up at the star-filled sky, letting her vision adjust to the darkness. The longer she lay there, the more stars she could see along with the hazy smear of millions of more stars that made up the Milky Way. "It's been so long since I've seen so many stars."

"I love to lay out here in the dark." Max chuckled, the sound deep and inviting. "I've been known to wake up out here after falling asleep in one of these chairs."

"Must be wonderful to live so far away from city lights."

"I love it," he said, simply.

"I can see why." She was staring up at the Big Dipper when a flash of light raced across the sky. "Was that—"

"A meteor?" he said. "Yes."

"I was going to say shooting star," she admitted. "But meteor is more realistic."

"My father always said that if you make a wish on a shooting star, your wish will come true."

Jane had already closed her eyes and made her wish. Only time would tell if it would come true.

"What did you wish for?" Max asked.

Jane opened her eyes and shot a glance his direction.

He'd turned his head to look in her direction.

"If I tell you, it won't come true," she said. Not that she would tell him. He didn't need to know that she'd wished he would ask her out on another date. There were a lot more things she could wish for, but she was starting with the short term. One step at a time.

Max reached for her hand and held it in his as they stared up at the stars.

Jane liked the feel of his calluses against her soft skin. This was a man who worked hard for a living. He lived an honest life, a life she'd love to be a part of.

If Leslie's matchmaking program held true, Jane's wish might come to pass, and she might eventually get to be a part of Max's life on the ranch.

A thrill of excitement and longing filled her soul and gave her hope.

Come on, Max. Ask me on that second date.

CHAPTER 8

BY THE TIME Max drove Jane back to the coffee shop in Austin, it was getting close to midnight. They'd lain in the darkness, holding hands for a long time.

Max wanted to do so much more, but he'd been afraid of scaring Jane off. When she'd come into the kitchen from her shower, wearing his T-shirt and gym shorts, he'd had to stand behind the counter eating cold fruit until his body calmed and his erection abated enough that he wouldn't embarrass himself.

For the love of football, her nipples had been taut, poking against the soft fabric of his favorite Aggies' T-shirt. He'd wanted to rip it off her body and taste those nipples himself, rather than satisfy his hunger with strawberries and cantaloupe.

The coffee house had long since closed, and the parking lot was deserted but for a lone white Lexus.

"Yours?" he asked.

She nodded. "Mine." With her key in hand, she started to get out of his truck.

Max touched her arm. "Wait."

Her brow furrowed.

"I'd like to think I can still be a gentleman, even though you ended up in the mud on our first date." He gave her a crooked grin and got out of the truck. Rounding the hood to the passenger side, he opened her door and helped her to the ground.

She stood with her key fob in her hand, dressed in her laundered jeans and slightly dingy white blouse. The mud stain hadn't quite washed out.

Neither said a word for a long, awkward moment.

Then she smiled up at him. "Thank you for the wonderful adventure."

He nodded. "Thank you for being a good sport about it."

She touched a hand to his chest. "I enjoyed it. That's the first adventure date I've ever been on." She leaned up on her toes and brushed his lips with hers. "I won't forget it."

When she started to drop back down, he captured her around her middle with one hand and curled the other behind her neck. "Neither will I." And he kissed her like he'd wanted to kiss her all evening. Hard, long and urgently.

She opened her lips to him, and he dove in, taking

her with all the passion he'd bottled up for the past few hours.

He wanted so much more. Standing in a parking lot in the middle of the night, a kiss was all he could expect.

Finally, he had to let her go.

He lifted his head, dazed with lust and longing. "I enjoyed our evening."

"Goodnight, Max."

"Goodnight, Jane."

She stepped away from him and hurried to her car.

Less than a minute later, she was gone.

For a long time, he stood near where he'd seen her into her car, staring at her disappearing taillights, his thoughts whirling in his head.

Then one came through the cacophony of images. He'd forgotten to get her freakin' phone number!

Max dove into his truck, revved the engine and took off after Jane.

Within minutes, he realized it was too late. She'd disappeared onto another road and blended into the traffic.

At a loss as to how to get hold of her, other than through the email system of BODS, Max dialed Tag's number.

"Dude, do you know what time it is?" Tag's groggy voice sounded over Max's truck speaker.

"I didn't get her damned phone number," Max cried.

"What? Whose phone number? Are you drunk? If you need someone to pick you up, call a taxi."

"I'm not drunk, but I'm in Austin, and I need a place to stay tonight." Max turned his truck around and headed for Tag's apartment.

"And you want to stay at my place? Why not Coop or Gage's place?"

"They're out on ranches, and you're in town."

"What if I'd had a woman here?" Tag argued.

Max snorted. "You haven't been on a date since I can remember. If I was a betting man, I'd say you're in love with someone you can't have, and you're abstaining until she's mentally or legally available."

"Shut up, Max. You don't know what you're talking about. And if you want to stay here, you'll keep your opinions to yourself."

"Struck a nerve?" Max chuckled. "I'm on my way. You'll be up with a cold beer?"

"I'll be up." Tag sighed. "The beer is cold."

Max parked in the lot of Tag's complex, locked his truck and took the stairs up to Tag's second floor apartment.

As Max raised his hand to knock, Tag opened the door and shoved an ice-cold longneck bottle of beer into his hand.

"Get in here, you're letting out all the AC." Tag grabbed his arm and pulled him inside. Dressed in gym shorts and a Lynyrd Skynyrd T-shirt, he padded barefooted into his living room and plopped down on the black leather sofa, propping his feet on the glass coffee table in front of him.

"Sit and spill," he said.

Max stood in the middle of the living room, shaking his head. "I don't know where to start." Then he downed half the bottle before he met Tag's gaze. "The date couldn't have gone worse."

"That bad?"

"No." He shook his head. "That good."

Tag scrubbed a hand down his face. "Wait, that doesn't make sense. Did you take her to a nice restaurant like we suggested?"

Max shook his head.

Tag sat forward. "You took her out to the ranch. Are you out of your mind? That's not what you do on a first date."

Max frowned. "I needed to know she was game for roughing it."

Tag crossed his arms over his chest. "I take it she wasn't."

"No, she was." Max stared at his friend, his eyes wide. "She showed up in blue jeans like I'd asked. And get this, she didn't wear any makeup. I didn't ask for that, but there she was, with no makeup."

"And she wasn't butt-ugly?"

"Not at all. She was fresh and clean and beautiful in her own way."

"Blond or brunette?" Tag asked.

"Blond."

"I thought you didn't like blondes."

"I thought so, too, but it didn't matter. It's what's inside that matters. I've known that all along."

Tag nodded. "That's right. Hair color is irrelevant. If she's good on the inside, she's good all over—blond, brunette, redhead, thin, chubby, short or tall."

"Exactly."

"And is she?" Tag asked.

"Is she what?"

Tag patted his chest. "Good on the inside?"

"I believe she is." Max took another long draw off his beer and shot a crooked grin Tag's way. "When I crashed my ATV in the creek, she bailed off hers, slid down the bank, and face-planted in the mud just to help me. Not many women would do that."

Tag blinked. "Wait. What? She slid down the bank and face-planted in the mud?" He laughed. "Oh, man, you blew it. Big time."

"You think?" Max frowned. "I helped her up and laid down in the creek with her to wash the mud off. Then she helped me by sitting with me on her four-wheeler to put weight on it so that we could drag the other one up to bank."

Tag groaned. "No, no, no. You did not ask her to add her weight to the back of the ATV." Tag shook his head back and forth. "You never talk weight around a woman."

"Why the hell not? And where are you finding all these rules about women? I swear you must have a playbook."

"You're how old?"

"Thirty-four. Why?"

"You'd think by now, you'd have a clue."

Max flipped him the bird.

Tag leaned forward. "Most women want to be treated like royalty. Like they're the most precious thing in your life, and you'll do anything to protect them from danger."

Max snorted. "If you're such an expert, why aren't you married? And I don't see any women lining up for the job of Mrs. Taggert Bronson."

"I'm not the one worried I won't get a second date." Tag crossed his arms over his chest. "How's your plan working out for you?"

"That's just it; I don't know. And I want to call and ask her out again, but two things are keeping me from it."

"Which are...?" Tag asked, eyebrows raised.

"I think she might say no."

"Not a reason to keep from calling," Tag said. "Next."

Heat rose in Max's cheeks. "I didn't get her number."

"You spent several hours with the woman, and you didn't get her number?"

"I didn't think about it until she'd driven off."

After he'd kissed her, and his vision and thoughts had become clouded with lust.

"You can contact her through the email the BODS system uses." Tag raised his hands, palms up. "What are you waiting for?"

"Emails are too impersonal. I want to hear her voice when she tells me no."

"Why are you so convinced she'll say no?"

"I kissed her before we parted."

"So?"

"No, I really kissed her."

"Again…so?"

"I didn't ask her permission, just laid one on her."

"Did she struggle?"

Max shook his head. "No."

"Did she tell you no or to back off?"

"No."

"Then what are you worried about?"

"That she might think I came on too strong, and she'll want nothing more to do with me."

"And this bothers you?" Tag grinned. "Are you falling for her?"

Max glared at Tag. "If I was, I sure as hell wouldn't tell you."

Tag's face split into a huge grin. "You are! Damn, I knew Leslie's program would find you the perfect match."

"Look, it's only a perfect match if it goes both ways. I'm not so sure she feels the same."

"Ha!" Tag pointed at him. "You are falling for her."

Max paced across the floor. "I don't know. So far, she's hitting all my buttons. She likes to cook, enjoys the outdoors. Hell, even my dog likes her. And my dog hasn't liked any of the women I've brought out to the ranch." He frowned. "For that matter, none of the women I've introduced to the ranch have come back for a second visit."

"Exactly my point. They didn't want to get caught up in your fantasy of being a rancher."

"Jane didn't seem to mind. I swear, she actually liked four-wheeling."

"Or she pretended to like it, to please you."

"You think?" Max pinched the bridge of his nose. "I don't know what to think."

Tag gave him a sly glance. "So, tell me about the kiss."

Max dropped his hand, heat climbing up his neck, filling his cheeks. "What kind of question is that? A gentleman doesn't kiss and tell."

Tag grinned. "Question is, did you get past first base?"

"None of your business," Max said. "Besides, a gentleman doesn't move that fast on a first date."

"So, you didn't get past first base." Tag laughed. "Why didn't you just say so?"

"You're missing the point of all of this."

"What? That you're a frustrated man who didn't

get past first base?" Tag grinned and ducked when Max launched a throw pillow at him.

"No," Max said. "The point is that I want to ask her out again, but I don't want to do that unless I know how she feels about our disastrous first date."

"And you want to call her and ask?" Tag's eyebrow rose. "You think she'd tell you if she hated it?"

"No." Max paced the floor, shoving a hand through his hair. "She wouldn't tell me." He stopped halfway across the room, spun and faced Tag. "But she'd tell Leslie."

Tag nodded. "Probably."

Max scooped Tag's cellphone off the end table beside him and shoved it toward Tag. "Call Leslie."

Tag took the phone, shaking his head. "I'm not calling Leslie. It's after midnight."

"Call her. Tell her...I don't know...tell her it's an emergency."

"The emergency being you've lost your mind?" Tag shook his head. "I'm not calling her."

"Then give me her number, and I'll call her." He held out his hand for the cellphone.

"I'm not giving you her number." Tag frowned. "You've completely lost it, dude."

"I need to know."

"It can wait until morning."

"No, it can't." Max crossed to stand in front of Tag. "Please. Call her. Blame it all on me for waking her up."

"Damn right, I'm blaming in on you," Tag muttered. "I'm beginning to think BODS is a bigger problem than I originally thought."

"You dragged all of us into this. The least you can do is make this one call for me."

"Okay, okay. But if she bites my head off, *you're* going to apologize to her." Tag brought up his contacts list and selected Leslie Lambert's number. "She's going to be mad if I wake her up." He shut up and listened. A moment later, he looked across at Max. "It rang once and went to her voicemail. She must be talking to someone else."

"Why didn't you leave a message?" Max asked.

"No need," Tag said. "I'll call back in a few minutes."

Max's heartbeat stuttered. "Who would Leslie be talking to this late at night?"

Max and Tag spoke at the same time, "Jane."

* * *

"Leslie, I'm sorry to be calling you so late, but I had to talk to someone." Jane hadn't waited until she'd gotten back to her house. As soon as she'd left Max in the parking lot of the coffee shop, she'd rang Leslie.

"It's okay. I wasn't sleeping anyway. I got hooked on a television show, and I've been binge-watching all the episodes." Leslie laughed. "I'm tucked into bed, wide awake and halfway through season three. So, thank you for saving me from spending the rest of the night wading through two more seasons."

Jane chuckled. "You sound like you need to use your own program to find your perfect match."

"No way. I'm still trying to get BODS off the ground. I don't have time for a relationship," Leslie said. "Besides, I had a good one and I'm not sure I'll find another match as perfect as my first husband."

"As a wise woman once said to me, you have to be open to the possibilities," Jane said.

Leslie laughed. "That's what I get for waxing poetic. How was your date with Max?"

Jane hesitated.

"That bad?" Leslie asked softly.

Jane sighed. "Not bad…but not good."

"Tell me all about it."

Jane could imagine Leslie settling back against her pillows. The image helped her open up about the afternoon and evening. She told her about the four-wheeler ride, the picnic and the mud bath, at which point, Leslie laughed.

"I'm sorry, but I can see you covered in mud, trying to impress a guy on the first date."

"It wasn't funny. I was a complete mess."

"Oh, sweetie, have you ever thought that maybe he liked that you weren't afraid to be a complete mess in front of him?" Leslie chuckled. "Face-plant in the mud. That's a new one for the book of fifty worst dates."

Jane's heart slipped into the bottom of her belly. "Tell me you're not writing that book."

Leslie chuckled. "No, dear. But, if I did, my dates would go first. Believe me, I've had worse."

"Worse than being covered in mud?"

Leslie snorted. "Yes. What happened after the mud incident?"

Jane went on to tell her about rinsing off in the creek, rescuing the drowned ATV and riding double all the way back to the barn.

"That doesn't sound awful. And he let you drive?" Leslie paused. "Which means he had his arms around you all the way back. How did that feel?"

Jane's body heated. "Other than being soaked to the skin...kind of wonderful."

"Perfect!" Leslie said. "I *knew* BODS could do it. The program works."

"But..."

"Uh-oh, we don't like buts," Leslie said. "But what?"

"But I don't know if he felt the same."

"What happened when you got back to the barn?"

Jane went into having showered, wearing his T-shirt, eating fruit and holding hands under the stars.

"Sounds like he moved past the mud bath," Leslie said. "The big question is, did he kiss you?"

Jane had avoided sharing those parts of the day. Sharing information about a kiss felt too personal.

"I'll take that as a yes," Leslie said. "Sounds to me like—" Leslie paused. "Wait, I'm getting a call."

"Who would be calling you at this hour, besides me?" Jane asked. As soon as the words were out of her mouth, the blood drained from her face, and she felt light-headed. Her fingers tightened on the steering wheel as she turned into her driveway, glad she'd made it home without crashing.

"It's Tag." Leslie laughed. "He's a friend of Max's. I wonder if Max called him." She shrugged. "I'll call him back. Now, where was I?"

Jane's head spun and her pulse raced. "You should answer that call."

"I was talking to you," Leslie said. "I'll call back when we're done here.

"We're done here. Really, you should answer." Jane's fingers squeezed the steering wheel so hard her knuckles turned white.

"Too late," Leslie said. "It must have gone straight to my voicemail."

Jane leaned her head against the headrest, forcing air in and out of her lungs. Had she known dating would cause this much stress, she might have stayed single for the rest of her life.

But now that she'd met Max, she didn't want to go back to her lonely existence. She wanted to see him again.

"Do you think he'll call me for another date?" Jane asked, her voice barely a whisper.

"Sweetie," Leslie answered. "How could he not? You're an amazing woman. Any man would be lucky to have you as part of his life."

"Even without makeup? And mud on my face, in my ears and the crevices of my nose?"

"You didn't whine or cry, did you?" Leslie asked.

"No," Jane said.

"All the more reason to fall in love with you," Leslie said. "Max struck me as a man who appreciates a strong woman."

"I don't think I came across as strong." Jane's lips twisted. "More like a big klutz."

"I doubt that."

"No, seriously, no one would suspect the Jane Gentry of yesterday was a world-renowned, graceful model. Did I tell you that I tripped and fell off the stage in Vegas?"

Leslie gasped. "No, you didn't. I'm surprised you didn't break anything. Those runways are usually pretty high off the ground."

"Had some hulk of a man catch me."

"Anyone interesting?"

"Not to me. He looked like a professional athlete. Athletes are more into themselves than a relationship. I'm getting too old to be some man's arm-candy."

"You are *not* too old," Leslie cried. "You haven't even turned thirty, yet."

"I will soon. And in modeling years, that's

ancient. It's a good thing I'm retiring after the Dallas Children's Hospital Charity Gala. That's my last gig."

"You're kidding, right?" Leslie asked. "The world will be a less beautiful place without you on the covers of my magazines."

"I need to make room for the younger models. Besides, I don't need the money. I've saved a lot of money, and I have an impressive portfolio."

Leslie laughed. "So, you're really going through with it? You're going to be a chef?"

"Yup. And write cookbooks," Jane said. "And I'm going to sample all of the things I put into that cookbook. No more starving myself to fit into ridiculous bikinis." Her voice trailed down into a whisper. "And I want a husband and children."

Leslie sighed. "Sounds like you have it all planned out. BODS is going to help you get there. I have a good feeling about you and Max."

"I know it's too soon to say anything. I'm afraid I'll jinx things," Jane said. "But I really like him. He's the kind of man who'll tell me like it is. An honest man I can trust. If he doesn't like me, I'll know soon enough."

"And if he does like you, when are you going to tell him who you really are? Sounds like he doesn't have a clue."

"He doesn't strike me as a man who follows the tabloids. I don't think he'll find out who I am. And I don't want him to know until we've known each other a little better."

"You know the longer you wait, the harder it'll be to tell him."

Jane nodded before she remembered Leslie couldn't see her. "I know. I didn't want to spoil the moment." She'd thought about telling him as they lay staring up at the stars. She'd even opened her mouth several times to bring it up, but she'd chickened out.

Holding out on him went against her grain. She valued honesty, yet she wasn't being honest with him. How would he feel if he knew she was a high-powered model, used to the limelight and followed by paparazzi?

"Is it wrong of me to want to be loved for me, not the fully made-up model?" she asked.

"No. But if Max is the one, he needs to know what he's getting himself into. Not just any man can handle celebrity life."

"But I'm retiring from that life."

Leslie snorted softly. "It will be a while before the public forgets about Angel Gentry. You're practically a household name. Women would follow you into your sixties and seventies just to see how you handle aging. You're an inspiration to many of us."

"Thank you, Leslie. But I just want to have a normal life with a husband and children before I'm too old to have children."

"Sweetie, you're far from too old."

"Now, I am. If it takes me more than one shot at this online dating, it could be years before I marry. I don't have many more years left that I can safely have kids."

"Having children is not guaranteed. Have you thought about that?"

Jane's heart squeezed hard in her chest. "I have. All the more reason to get moving on the plan to marry and start trying to get pregnant. I want children, but if I can't have them naturally, I'll adopt. I might adopt even if I have children of my own. There are plenty of kids in foster care who need good homes."

"It's going to happen for you, Jane. And if Max is the one, I'll help you two any way I can. But the attraction has to be on both sides."

Jane sighed. "I know."

"All you can do is wait for him to call you for the second date. Or *you* can call *him*."

"I was hoping *he'd* call *me*." She grimaced. "But I didn't give him my number."

"Do you give me permission to give him your number?"

"Yes!"

"If he asks for it, I will."

"Thank you, Leslie. Without you and BODS, I don't think I'd stand a chance. Put me on a runway, dress me in the latest fashion and I'll perform. I'm just not good at this whole dating gig."

"You're fine. And I bet he'll email or call you in the next twenty-four hours to arrange that next meeting." Leslie chuckled. "Hopefully, not on the ranch."

"Actually, I loved being on the ranch. But maybe not sliding down a hill and landing in the mud."

"Got my fingers crossed for you."

Jane hit the button for her garage door, waited for it to open and then pulled in. As she got out of her car, she found herself crossing her fingers and sending a silent prayer to the matchmaking gods…

Call me, Max Smith!

CHAPTER 9

"WHAT DID YOU FIND OUT?" Max sat at Tag's dining table, a fresh cup of coffee warming his hand.

"Can I start the caffeine IV before you drill me with questions?" Tag grumbled.

"I've been up for hours, grinding my teeth," Max admitted. "I almost woke you a dozen times. Be glad I didn't."

"You should be glad you didn't." Tag plunked a coffee mug on the counter and filled it to the brim. "I keep a loaded gun beneath my pillow."

"Good to know." Max waited for Tag to take a seat opposite him. "I heard you talking after I called it a night. Did Leslie call after I hit the sack?"

Tag lifted his mug and took his first sip before responding, "She did."

"What did she say?"

"She said she talked to Jane."

Max sat forward, every nerve on edge. "And?"

"She said Jane was okay with the date."

"Okay?" Max sat back in his seat. "Only okay?"

"What did you expect? You dunked her in the mud on your first date." Tag yawned. "Then you kept your best friend up until all hours whining about how you didn't think she'd go out with you again."

Max pushed his hand through his hair. "Just okay." He shook his head. "What are the chances she'd go out with me again to make it up to her?"

"Slim to none?" Tag offered.

Max glared at his friend. "You're not helping."

Tag lifted his cellphone, brought up the screen, touched a few keys and sat back. "You're welcome."

"For what?" Max wasn't feeling very thankful at the moment.

"I just shared the phone number Leslie sent."

"Phone number for who?" Max said. "I'm not interested in dating anyone else. You can tell Leslie that yourself."

"Then I don't suppose you'll want the number I sent."

"I don't need Leslie's number, now."

"No, dumbass. It's Jane's number." Tag laughed. "You're wound tighter than a baby rattler with a new button on his tail."

Max's cellphone pinged with an incoming text

message. He grabbed the phone and stared down at the shared contact information for Jane Gentry. When he started to touch the number and call her, a hand shot out to stop him.

Max glared at Tag's hand on his arm.

"Have you thought about what you're going to say or do?" Tag asked.

"I'm going to ask her out again," Max said and shook off Tag's hand.

"Dude, you need a better plan than your last one, or you'll lose her. You're lucky she'd giving you a second chance to treat her right."

As much as he wanted to call Jane that very second, Max knew Tag was right. "What do you suggest?"

"Do something normal. Meet her for coffee. Take her to a movie. Make reservations for a fancy dinner Austin. Show her you want to be with her, without testing her ability to rough it on a ranch."

"What if she says no to another date?" Max asked, staring at her number as if willing her to say yes.

"She gave Leslie permission to give you her phone number. She's not going to say no to a second date. But she might say no to a third if you don't get it right this time."

Max dropped the cellphone onto the table and threw up his hands. "Gah! How do people date? I need a damned playbook."

Tag smiled. "Dating can be like football. You have

to practice enough with your receiver to feel comfortable that he can catch whatever you throw his way, right?"

Max frowned. "What does that have to do with dating?"

"You need to go out several times on neutral ground to get comfortable with each other, before you move on to more intricate plays." Tag's eyes narrowed. "Get my drift?"

"I think so," Max said, though he wasn't entirely sure. "Go on."

"Invite her out for coffee. Let her get used to you and your dumb jokes."

"Hey." Max punched Tag in the arm. "My jokes aren't any dumber than yours."

Tag rubbed the spot Max had punched. "My point exactly. She has to be willing to put up with your warped sense of humor. That takes practice."

"Okay. I'll ask her out for coffee." Max lifted the cellphone.

Tag put his hand over it. "One play is not an entire plan. Have it all laid out and play through to the Hail Mary pass at the end."

"Coffee this afternoon. A movie the next night. Dinner on Thursday?" Max raised his eyebrows. "Is that thinking far enough ahead?"

"Yes. If you think she's the one for you, you need to introduce her to your friends."

Max shook his head and held up his hands. "No

way. There are two of you still single and on the prowl. I'm not exposing her to you and Sean and have you poach her right out from under me."

"If we're able to poach her, she wasn't that interested in you to begin with." Tag raised his eyebrows. "Isn't it better to know that now than after you're married?"

Max studied his friend through slitted eyes. "I'm not so sure."

"I promise not to hit on her." He grinned. "I can't vouch for Sean. We could have a night out with the gang at the Ugly Stick Saloon. It's far enough away from Austin we won't have to put up with the weekend traffic."

"They usually have good music," Max considered. "I taught her how to two-step. It would be a good time for her to try out her new skills." He clapped his hands together. "Coffee, movie, dinner and dancing. That about cover it?"

Tag nodded. "To start with. If you last an entire week, you might have a chance with her."

Again, Max raised his cellphone.

Again, Tag put his hand over Max's. "You might want to wait until this afternoon before you call her. You don't want to appear too desperate."

"I am desperate," Max said. "I want to see her again...in this century. If I wait until this afternoon to call, what am I supposed to do in the meantime?"

Tag gave him a pointed stare. "You could go home and get a shower. It's not like you're going to take her out tonight. That's way over the top far too soon."

Frustration bubbled up inside Max. "This had better work."

Tag held up his hands. "These are all suggestions that may or may not work. Just like any play on the football field, you have to be flexible and adjust when necessary. The main thing is to treat her like she's special. Not like she's a used car being test driven." Tag frowned at Max. "And don't push the physical side. You'll know when she's ready."

Max's head spun. He wasn't new to dating, but he was new to dating for his future. He didn't want to blow it. But he wasn't sure he was cut out to be as patient as Tag's suggestions would require.

"If calling now is too soon and will make me look desperate, how long should I wait?"

"I'd give it until later today. Not too long that she feels like you've moved on, but long enough to make her wonder what she missed and might want to see more of." Tag clapped a hand to Max's shoulder. "Relax. It'll all work out."

Max wasn't at all sure it would. Not if he had to follow a playbook in a game he felt was out of his league.

* * *

"You did give him my cellphone number, didn't you?" Jane asked Leslie halfway through the next day.

"I gave it to Tag," Leslie said. "He promised to pass it on to Max."

"Is there any way to know whether or not he's done that?" Jane didn't want to nag, but the suspense was killing her.

Leslie laughed. "I asked Tag. He said he sent it in a text to Max. Give him time. He'll call."

Jane hadn't slept much the night before. By the time she went to bed, it was almost two o'clock in the morning. Sleep hadn't come until an hour later, and she'd woken up by seven after dreaming she'd missed a phone call from Max.

She'd sat up in bed and checked her cellphone. No calls. The only people who had her cellphone number were her closest friends, her mother and her agent, Layne Sanders.

With adrenaline running rampant through her veins, she had no choice but to get up and get moving.

Jane went for a jog, her cellphone strapped to her arm, earbuds in her ears. If Max called, she'd be there to answer, but she wouldn't be mooning around the house.

She'd gone three miles before the Texas heat got to her, and she headed back to the comfort of her airconditioned house.

Though she had a maid to clean once a week, Jane

couldn't sit around and do nothing all day. She spent the next two hours going through the clothing in her closets, weeding out items she hadn't worn in the past year. She shoved them into a huge garbage bag and hauled them off to the women's shelter thrift store to donate.

When she returned, she went for a swim, keeping her head above the water at all times so she wouldn't miss the phone ringing.

She'd completed twenty laps and still Max hadn't called. Her stomach rumbled, reminding her she hadn't had breakfast and noon was long past.

Jane entered her kitchen and looked around with a critical eye. If she kept the house, she would completely remodel the kitchen to be more user-friendly. But for now, she pulled out the recipe file she'd kept over the years. She'd promised herself she'd try different dishes once she wasn't modeling anymore and could finally eat things that were loaded with carbs and calories without worrying about gaining a pound or two.

Two hours later, she had four dozen chocolate chip cookies cooling on racks across every bit of counterspace she had in her kitchen.

"What the hell am I going to do with four dozen cookies?" she said out loud.

As if in answer to her question, her cellphone rang.

It took her a few moments to locate it beneath a

dishtowel. When she did, her heart sank a little. The caller ID on the screen indicated Leslie Lambert.

"Hi, Leslie."

"Has he called?"

"No." Jane glanced around at the cookies, tears welling in her eyes. She would not cry. She'd only just met the man, and they hadn't been together for more than about four hours. That was not enough to form a lasting relationship.

"What's wrong with the man?" Leslie asked. "Tag said he enjoyed his day with you. I thought by now he'd have called and set up your next date."

Jane sighed. "Maybe he didn't enjoy it as much as I did. Face it, I've been working since I was fourteen. Other than modeling, what do I have to offer?"

"You're a wonderful person," Leslie argued. "And you're game to try anything, as evidenced by the insane first date he took you on."

"I might not have measured up. He probably wants a farm girl who knows one end of a horse from another."

Leslie snorted. "You can learn all that. It's not rocket science."

"No, but why teach someone who has never lived on a ranch when you can find plenty of willing women who have?"

"He'll call. He might have had something come up. It is Monday and a workday. I bet he calls this evening. Don't give up hope."

"I won't," Jane said, though she was halfway there already.

She ended the call and started bagging cookies. She'd give some to Leslie and take the rest to the fire station. Surely, the firefighters would like some home-baked cookies.

She'd bagged two of the four dozen cookies when her phone rang again. Jane's heart leaped. She dropped the bag she'd been stuffing to check the caller ID.

Layne Sanders. Her agent.

"Hi, Layne." Jane balanced her cellphone between her chin and shoulder and continued to stuff cookies into plastic bags. "What's up?"

"I wanted to see if you'd changed your mind about retiring?"

"Nope," she said. "I'm out of the modeling business. I have enough other interests to keep me busy and off the runway."

"Are you sure? I have a great opportunity in Paris next month," he said. "They're asking for you."

"We've been through this. I'm done. Don't commit me for anything else."

"You're still on for the charity event in Dallas, aren't you? They're counting on you. They've got a lot of celebrities lined up to be there and are expecting the donations to far exceed last year's event."

Jane sighed. "I told you I wouldn't let the kids

down. But it's the last modeling assignment for me. You've been really great to work with, but I'm tired, and I want a real life. If I don't start now, it won't happen."

"I understand. I get it." Jane could hear the tap, tap, tap of a pen on Layne's wood desktop. "I just hate losing you as a client."

"And I'm sorry to let you down. I know you're going to lose the commissions, but I'll be sure to recommend you to any up and coming stars that shine my way."

"There will never be another Angel Gentry."

"There will be dozens," she assured him. "By the way, do you like chocolate chip cookies?"

"Of course. They're the family favorite," he answered. "Why?"

"No reason," she said. "Give your wife my love and kiss the kids for me."

"Will do, Jane. Gonna miss you. And if you decide retirement isn't all it's cracked up to be ..."

"You'll be the first one I call right after my therapist." She chuckled as she ended the call. Then she set aside a bag of cookies she'd box and overnight to Layne and his family in LA.

After she'd packaged all the cookies, she filled the sink full of soapy water and washed the pans and racks. With her arms up to her elbows in suds and the water running, she didn't hear her cellphone ringing until it had rung a few times.

When she finally did, she dove for it on the counter behind her, sloshing soap bubbles across the floor.

The number on the screen wasn't familiar. Her heart raced and her breath caught in her throat as she answered, "Hello."

"Jane?" Max's deep voice sounded in her ear, causing all kinds of sensory stimulation to her head, her hand and her entire body.

Her tongue tied as she struggled to form a coherent thought. "Yes," she managed to eke out.

"Max here."

She held the cellphone away from her face and cleared her throat before responding in as calm a manner as she could manage, "Hi, Max."

"Are you recovered from your adventure on the ranch?" he asked.

"Nothing to recover from," she said. "I had a nice time."

"Nice might be stretching it, but I'm glad you did." He hesitated, but then continued, "I'm calling to see if you'd like to get some coffee."

"I have coffee here at my house," she said. Having waited all day by the phone, she had no qualms over making him work for it...but not too hard.

"I mean, would you like to go get coffee with me tomorrow morning."

"Don't you have to work?" she asked.

"Uh. I have flexible hours," he said. "I'm there

when I need to be," Max explained. "That could be pulling an all-nighter with a sick horse or working through the weekend to get the hay in before it rains."

"I see. In that case, yes. I'd like to have coffee with you tomorrow."

"Okay then. Want to meet at the same place I picked you up yesterday?"

"That will work," she said, feeling awkward and wishing she didn't.

"I'll see you there at nine o'clock?"

"Make it eight. I like my coffee first thing in the morning," Jane said and ended the call before she chickened out and told Max she'd agree to any time, just to see him. If he'd wanted to meet in an hour, she'd have dropped everything and jumped in her car.

Wow. When had she become desperate?

When she'd met a man who'd taken her four-wheeling and taught her how to two-step, all on the same date.

She'd go back out to the ranch and roll in the mud all over again, if that was what he wanted. Hell, the man had asked her out for coffee after seeing her covered in mud from head to toe. He couldn't have been too frightened. And he'd held her hand in the starlight.

Warmth spread through her at the memory of his big, work-roughened hand holding hers.

Happiness bubbled up inside of her, and Jane spun around with a little squeal of delight. Then she grabbed her phone and called Leslie.

CHAPTER 10

Max arrived thirty minutes early at the designated coffee shop. For the next ten minutes he drove around the block several times, feeling ridiculous. Finally, he parked in front of the coffee shop and watched people go in and out and pull through the drive-through window.

Eight o'clock came and went. By five minutes past the hour, Max was convinced Jane wasn't coming. He worried she'd been in a wreck trying to get to the coffee shop during rush-hour traffic. All manner of scenarios roiled through his mind until he lifted his cellphone, ready to call 911 and report a missing person.

Then her white Lexus pulled in beside his truck, and she got out.

A rush of relief rolled over him, and he dropped

down out of the cab of his pickup. "Good morning," he said and drank in the sight of her.

She'd worn a soft, powder blue T-shirt dress that hung past her knees and had a belt cinched at her tiny waist. Her hair was pulled up in a loose bun at the crown of her head with loose tendrils framing her face.

Again, she'd worn no makeup and didn't need to. Her violet eyes shone from her pale face, and her smile lit the morning.

"Good morning," she said, ducking her head, her cheeks turning a light shade of pink.

He liked the color rising in her cheeks and wanted to be the one who always made her smile. He cupped her elbow and guided her toward the door. "I didn't think to ask, but you do like coffee, don't you?"

"If I didn't, would you think less of me?" she asked and tilted her head to the side to look up at him.

"Not at all. Sometimes, I wish I wasn't so dependent on it to get me going in the morning."

"I'm sure your form of coffee is different than mine. I like mine fully loaded with everything and very little coffee."

He nodded. "And I like mine black, one teaspoon of sugar." He opened the door and held it as she walked through.

Jane turned to him. "Did you recover your four-wheeler from the creek side?"

"I did. The carburetor will have to be rebuilt, but it'll run again soon."

"I'm glad. I can imagine ATVs can be quite useful on a ranch. They aren't as temperamental as horses."

"I don't know. I've had some that waited until I was the farthest away possible from the barn when they quit working. Of course, I was alone those times and had to walk all the way back from where I'd left the ATV." He smirked. "But then I've had a horse throw me just about as far from the ranch house and high-tail it back to the barn without me. So, yes, in that respect, an ATV can be less temperamental than a horse."

They stood in line and placed their orders, then waited a few steps away for the barista to create their coffee.

Once they had their drinks in hand, Max turned and started toward the far-right corner of the little shop. He glanced at a poster on the wall and nearly dropped his scalding hot coffee in the middle of the floor.

He caught it before it fell or spilled, but he couldn't believe what he was seeing.

On the wall hung a large poster of him in his Texas Ramblers NFL football jersey with his number 57 written in giant blue letters across his chest. He remembered that particular photo shoot, holding a cup of coffee in one hand and his helmet in the other. He'd been paid well for that endorsement, and he genuinely liked the coffee. He just wished the ad campaign hadn't started until after his coffee date with Jane.

Positioning his body between Jane and the poster, he prayed she didn't see him in all his football gear. He didn't want her to know he was something more than a simple rancher. He wasn't ready to expose that part of his life to her. He wanted her to like him for the man he was in the blue jeans, not the jersey.

Maneuvering her to a seat facing away from the advertisement, Max held her chair and waited for her to take her seat.

Once she was seated, he took his seat, trying to focus on her and not the fact his face was posted on the wall behind Jane, larger than life and staring at him accusingly. He should confess. He just wasn't ready.

They spent a nice hour talking about the ranch, the work he was doing to rebuild the ATV engine after it had been waterlogged and the fact Jane had baked cookies the day before. She'd brought him a tin of them, and they enjoyed eating them as they drank their coffee. He relaxed and almost forgot about the poster.

When the hour was over, Max suggested they go for a walk in a nearby park. Getting her out of the coffee shop proved more of a challenge and a young male barista, arriving for his shift, nearly blew Max's cover.

"Hey, are you the guy on the poster?" the kid behind the counter asked.

Max shook his head. "Don't know what you're talking about."

"You look just like Moose Smithson from the Texas Ramblers."

He gave the guy a crooked grin. "I get that a lot, but nope. Not me." He hooked Jane's elbow and hustled her past the counter and outside the building before she had a chance to look at the poster on the wall. He didn't breathe until they'd reached his truck.

He helped her up into the passenger seat and rounded the other side to climb behind the wheel.

"You do have a striking resemblance to the football player on the poster in the coffee shop," Jane said as she fastened her seatbelt across her lap.

Max shrugged. "What can I say? We have the same facial structure." Internally, he kicked himself. He should have taken that opportunity to tell her the truth.

A quick glance at Jane reminded him that she was a sweet, quiet woman who probably wouldn't like the lifestyle of a celebrity.

When he wasn't performing organized publicity stunts, Max worked hard to avoid recognition. Paparazzi seemed to always be where he'd least expect them. His truck was registered under his ranch's name, a name that had nothing to do with Maxwell "Moose" Smithson, the NFL football player. He kept his private life as private as he could.

Being in Austin left him open to "sightings". Thankfully, most people didn't recognize him without his jersey and pads. Unless he happened to be standing next to a poster with his face on it in a coffee shop.

The walk in the park was very nice. As they walked, he held her hand. When they came to the small lake at the center of the park, he led her to a park bench. They sat and talked about the ducks and geese on the water, the weather and the best place to go to watch the bats fly out of their caves by the thousands.

He didn't want the time to end, but eventually, they got up to walk back to the truck. He drove her to the coffee shop and helped her down from the passenger seat.

For a long moment, they stood toe to toe, holding hands.

"I enjoyed coffee and the walk," she said.

"I did, too." He lifted one of her hands to his lips and brushed the backs of her knuckles with a light kiss. "Thank you."

Though he wanted to pull her into his arms and crush her to him, he stepped back, allowing her to walk to her car. As he held her door for her, she slid into the driver's seat. "I'll call you," he said.

She smiled up at him. "I'd like that."

He closed the door and stood there like a damned lump while Jane drove away.

Why did dating have to take so long?

The young man who'd spotted him earlier emerged from the coffee shop with the poster in his hands. "It's you. I just know it's you."

"Hold on." Max shot a glance toward Jane's car. She had just pulled out of the parking lot onto the busy road. After she'd turned the next corner, he returned his attention to the young man holding the poster and a pen.

"Could I get your autograph?"

"Sure."

"I told Beth it was you. I'd know Moose Smithson anywhere. I'll never forget that Hail Mary you threw at your last Super Bowl. It was amazing."

"Thank you." Max took the pen. "What's your name?"

"Jason. But if you could sign it to my father, I know he'd get a huge kick out of it. He'll be green with envy that I met Moose Smithson. I can't wait to tell him."

"Your father's name?" Max asked.

"Charles."

Max signed the poster to Charles and scribbled his signature across one corner. He added a post-script, *Jason's a good son.*

"Thank you, Mr. Smithson," Jason said. "Beth thought she recognized your girlfriend, but she couldn't put her finger on her name." He snorted. "But you're hard to miss. I can't believe I've met Moose Smithson."

Unfortunately, what Jason said was true. Being a big guy was part of playing football, which also made Max stand out. Thus, the reason for wearing sunglasses or hats when he was out in public. Max hadn't expected to walk into a coffee shop with a poster of him hanging on the wall.

He really needed to tell Jane the truth about himself. And he would...just not right now. They were getting along so well, and he wanted to see where the relationship would go over the next few days.

If BODS was truly the matchmaker of all time, Jane could be his future bride. He didn't want to mess up his chances of that happening. Max could almost hear the wedding march playing, and it didn't scare him as much as he thought it would. He loved how relaxed and natural he felt with Jane. She wasn't one of those high-maintenance women like he'd dated throughout his professional football career. She didn't hide behind layers of makeup and fancy clothing. She was...Jane.

He climbed into his truck, lifted his cellphone and called her. So what if it was so soon after leaving her. He couldn't wait to see her again.

· · ·

JANE WAS HALFWAY BACK to her house when the call came through on her cellphone. She glanced at the caller ID on the screen and laughed, delighted he'd called so soon after leaving her. She had wanted to dial his number as soon as she'd pulled out of the parking lot, but she didn't want to appear too eager. Leslie had cautioned her to play a little hard to get. Not too much, but enough to make the man want her all the more.

She let the cellphone ring three times before she answered with a chuckle. "Did you lock yourself out of your truck?"

"No," he said. "But I just remembered, I didn't ask when we could see each other again."

"I don't know," she said. "How's next week?"

"How about tomorrow night? I could take you out on a real date and treat you to a real dinner."

"Hmmm. I liked our not-so-real date."

"I'd like to show you I can be a gentleman when I want to be." He sighed into the phone. "And you make me want to be."

"Really? I'd rather make you want to wear blue jeans and ride ATVs."

"You do that already, but I owe you a nice dinner where there's no chance of falling in the mud."

She laughed, her chest swelling with warmth and more. "Okay. Tomorrow it is."

"I'll even pick you up this time."

She hesitated. He was a rancher. Angel Gentry

owned a swanky house in one of the most affluent neighborhoods of Austin. How would she explain that Plain Jane lived there? "I don't want you to go so far out of your way. I know you'll be coming in from out of town. Let me meet you at the restaurant."

"Are you sure you're not hiding a husband somewhere?"

She snorted. "Hardly." Thus, the reason for going with Leslie's online dating service. Jane hadn't had time to meet and marry anyone. "I live in a gated community and it's more hassle than it's worth to bring someone through the gate when I can get in and out on my own."

"Then we'll meet at the restaurant."

"Which one?" she asked.

"Are you up for Italian?"

"Always," she answered.

"Great," he said. "Then we'll meet at Riomaggiore. Have you heard of it?"

Not only had she heard of it, she'd worked a private fashion show for charity there. Plates had sold for one thousand dollars, and all had been bought by local Austin socialites and celebrities. She almost asked Max to pick a different location, but she'd just told him she loved Italian.

Short of sounding like a fool, she sucked it up and vowed to cover her face with sunglasses and wear her hair long and curly. In all her modeling, she'd straightened her hair or worn it slicked back.

"I've heard of Riomaggiore. What time?"

"I made the reservation for seven o'clock."

"You were that sure I'd agree to go out to dinner with you?" Jane asked.

"Not at all. But I knew if I wanted to get a reservation for tomorrow night, I had to make it last night."

"Wow. You had all this planned out?"

"I didn't know if you'd go with me, but I made the plans in case you decided I was worth the risk."

Oh, he was definitely worth the risk. "I'm impressed."

"Don't be. I had to make up for taking you mud riding on the ranch."

"Really, Max, I loved it. I'd never been on an ATV before I met you. Now, I'm looking forward to doing it again."

"And I'll take you, again." He paused. "After I show you that I can be a gentleman."

"I thought you were the perfect gentleman on the ranch," she insisted. "And you taught me how to two-step."

"Without music, in the dust," he reminded her.

"I thought it was perfect." Her voice lowered. "Just the two of us. No one butting in or bothering us." She couldn't remember the last time she'd felt so free and easy. And it was all because Max had taken her on a picnic out in the middle of nowhere.

To her, it had been perfect.

"Still," he said. "I want to show you that I can take a lady on a real date and treat her like she's special."

"Have you ever considered that someone might like to be treated like a normal person?" Being placed on a pedestal wasn't all it was cracked up to be. She could never be herself. As a model, she'd always been pretending to be someone she wasn't.

She wouldn't trade her life up to that moment for anything but, going forward, she was ready to move on to the next phase.

"I'll be at Riomaggiore at seven o'clock, tomorrow night," she said.

"I'll see you there," Max said. "And Jane?"

"Yes?"

"Thank you for a beautiful day."

"I should thank you. It's been a long time since I took a day off and just did something strictly for me."

"I have a confession to make," Max added.

Jane's belly clenched. She knew she should give him her own confession, but time had gone by without opening up about her real profession and the fact she had a load of money.

"Look, Max, you don't have to confess to anything. We all have our skeletons in our closets. I don't have to hear about yours." *And I don't want to tell you mine.*

"I wanted to kiss you this morning," Max said softly.

Jane's breath caught in her throat. "You did?"

"I did," he said.

"Then why didn't you?" she asked.

"I didn't want to scare you off."

"You wouldn't have scared me off." She'd wanted him to kiss her again—in the coffee shop, on their walk, when they stood in the parking lot before she'd driven off. She'd wanted to kiss him so very much.

He sighed into her ear. "I'm trying very hard to be a gentleman. I don't want to rush you like I did on our first date."

"Well, I have a confession, too," she said, her heart racing and her body on fire.

He chuckled. "Oh, yeah?"

"Uh-huh." She paused. "I wanted to kiss you, too." Her foot slipped off the accelerator. Jane had half a mind to turn around and drive back to that coffee shop and show him just how much she wanted to kiss him.

The red light in front of her turned green. A car behind her honked. She pressed her foot on the gas pedal, sending her Lexus shooting forward.

No, she couldn't rush back to the coffee shop just for a kiss, though her body and lips ached to do so. She and Max had a date for the next night. She'd claim that kiss then. Good Lord, she'd have to wait through the entire meal, choking down food she could care less about when all she could focus on was his mouth and the burning desire to kiss him.

"I'll see you tomorrow night," she said, her voice husky with lust.

"Until then," he said and ended the call.

Jane gripped the steering wheel so hard, her knuckles turned white. A wave of desire rushed over her, making her so hot and bothered, she wondered if she'd make it back to her house without coming apart.

She did make it through the gate and into her garage. When she got out of her car, she went straight for her swimming pool, stripping off her clothing until all she wore was her bra and panties. Then she dove in, letting the cool, clear water tamp down the raging hunger building inside.

Holy hell. How would she control herself at dinner the following night, knowing he wanted to kiss her? During the drive from the coffee shop to her house, Jane's cravings had gone from a simple kiss to a full-on, drag-him-to-the-bedroom-and-throw-him-on-the-bed desire.

After several laps back and forth across the pool, she'd worked her muscles and burned off some of the adrenaline raging through her system. When she emerged, she grabbed a towel, wrapped it around her body, collected her discarded clothing and hurried into the house.

A quick glance at the clock on the wall made her groan. Barely past one o'clock and she wouldn't see Max for another thirty hours.

Was this what it was like to fall in love? Wanting to be with that person twenty-four-seven? She moaned again and headed for the shower. Angel Gentry was a high-powered, former model with global business interests. Surely, she could keep Jane Gentry occupied for the next thirty hours with real work and beauty rest.

Only twenty-nine hours, fifty-five minutes and thirty seconds to go.

CHAPTER 11

MAX ARRIVED at Riomaggiore a whopping thirty minutes early and sat in his truck with the AC cranked up to full blast to keep from sweating in his tailored suit.

For the past thirty hours, he'd thrown himself into ranch work, wearing himself out the day before in order to sleep that night.

Earlier on this day, he'd mucked the horses' stalls, fixed a hinge on one of the gates and called it a day just after noon. He didn't want to be worn out when he arrived at the restaurant.

Despite working so hard, he'd dreamed about Jane. The dreams had been so vivid and erotic, he worried it would show on his face when they met that night.

He'd blown right past wanting to kiss her to wanting to make love to her. Holding back would be difficult. He hoped that being in a fancy restaurant, surrounded by fancy people, he would be uncomfortable enough to keep it cool.

Max glanced at the pale pink corsage lying on the seat beside him. It matched the bud on his lapel. Maybe it was overkill, but he wanted to prove to her that he could be that gentleman who would treat her like the princess she deserved to be.

He hoped Tag was correct in assuming all women wanted to be treated like a princess. Jane hadn't come off like that, but what did Max know?

Jane pulled up in her white Lexus, fifteen minutes early and parked beside his truck.

Max grabbed the corsage and leaped out of his truck. He stood for a full second, straightening his coat and tie, getting his pulse under control, before he rounded the hood of her car and opened her door.

He held out his hand. She placed hers in his and he pulled her to her feet.

She wore a spaghetti-strap, white dress that hugged her torso like a second skin and flared at her hips, falling softly around her thighs to her knees. On her feet, she wore a pair of strappy white sandals that showed off her pale pink, painted toenails. She smiled up at him. "Hey."

"Hey," he said.

Her gaze raked him from head to toe. "You clean up well for a cowboy."

He smiled. "You, too, for a woman who likes to go mudding."

She laughed and nodded toward the corsage in his hand. "Is that for me?"

He glanced at his hand. "It is. Do you want me to do the honors?"

She gave a brief nod. "I trust you."

Her words kicked him in the gut. He was glad she trusted him not to poke her with the pin. At the same time, a wash of guilt rippled through him. Would she trust him once she found out he'd been holding out on her about who he really was?

He moved closer, slipped his fingers beneath the fabric of her dress, his knuckles brushing against the swell of her breast. For a moment, he felt light-headed, all his blood rushing south into his groin. If they were further along in their relationship, he'd suggest they skip dinner and go straight to his house where they could make love into the night.

But they were still new to each other. Max didn't know just how committed Jane was to their budding romance. He could be leaps and bounds ahead of her and scare her off by moving too fast.

Carefully, he pushed the pin through the stem and fabric, securing the corsage. Again, his knuckles skimmed across her breast as he removed his hand from behind the fabric and dropped it to his side.

He glanced into her pretty, violet eyes, noticing for the first time that she'd worn a light layer of makeup on her cheeks and eyelids. It accentuated without covering her natural beauty. Her hair lay in soft curls to her shoulders, with tendrils cupping her cheeks.

"You're beautiful," he said softly and bent to kiss her lightly on her lips. With his lips still hovering over hers, he sighed. "I've wanted to do that since the last time we were together, thirty hours ago."

"I've wanted you to do that for the past thirty hours." She leaned up on her toes and pressed her lips to his, opening her mouth to let him in. Her tongue met his in a light dance that held the promise of more to come.

Someone honked in the street behind them, shaking Max from the trance he'd fallen into while kissing Jane.

"We'd better go inside before the Texas heat melts me in this suit." He held out his arm.

Jane hooked her hand through his elbow and let him lead her into the restaurant. "Who knew a rancher would have a suit like that in his closet," she commented. "It fits you to perfection."

"I'm a big guy. I couldn't buy one off the rack. I had to have it tailored."

"Your tailor did good." She squeezed his arm.

"Have you been here before?" he asked.

Jane nodded. "I have, but it's been a few months."

"Good, then you can tell me what's good on the menu. It's all in Italian."

She smiled. "I can do that."

"Do you speak Italian?" he asked.

"No, but I've spent enough time in Europe to learn how to order food in a few different languages."

"Europe?" He glanced down at her, aware of how much he still didn't know about her. "Well, I guess that makes sense, since you were in the fashion merchandising industry."

She nodded, her gaze on the maître d'.

The man was dressed in a black tuxedo, with a white cummerbund. He dipped his head and rolled his hand. "Welcome to Riomaggiore, Mr. Smithson."

Max cringed. He'd had to make the reservation in his real name, not in the short version of his last name he'd used on his BODS application. He hoped Jane hadn't noticed the difference. If she had, she didn't mention it.

They were led to their table in a quiet corner of the restaurant.

The maître d' draped their napkins across their laps, placed their menus in their hands and left them with, "Your waiter will be with you momentarily."

No sooner had he left their table, than their waiter appeared. Dressed in a black suit with a red tie, their waiter gave a slight bow. "Mr. Smithson." He nodded toward Jane. "Ms. Gentry, pleasure to see you again."

Jane's cheeks filled with color. "Thank you," she said and ducked her head behind her menu.

Max ordered a bottle of wine and the waiter left to get it.

"You must have made an impression on the waiter and the maître d' for them to remember you after a couple of months," Max commented.

Jane gave him a little smile. "I must have left a large tip."

A moment later, a dark-haired man approached the table, smiling effusively. "Welcome to Riomaggiore," he said with an Italian accent. "It is our pleasure to serve two such distinguished guests. Your patronage is greatly appreciated. I'm *Signor* Mateo, the owner. Please let me or my staff know of anything we can do to make your visit *bellissimo*."

Max wished he'd made it clear to the person taking his reservation that he wanted them to be discreet about their visit.

Heads turned in their direction.

Max nodded and smiled at the owner. "Thank you."

Once the owner left, Max shot a glance toward Jane. She lowered her menu and smiled at the waiter approaching with the bottle of wine.

He poured a little in one glass.

Max tasted and nodded.

The waiter poured more wine into his glass then in Jane's and left.

Jane held up her glass, her cheeks a little flushed. "To us getting to know each other better."

"To us." Max said, muttering beneath his breath, "A little sooner than expected." He tipped his glass and downed a hefty swallow.

Jane lowered her glass. "Did you say something?"

He smiled. "Is the wine to your taste?"

"It's perfect." She sipped again.

The rest of the meal went well. The wait staff didn't bother them or ask for autographs, much to Max's relief.

Jane ordered for them. The chicken marsala was cooked to perfection.

Max ate what he could, his gut twisting as he worried someone else might recognize him and make a big deal. So far, it didn't appear as though Jane had noticed the fuss the staff made over them.

Near the end of their meal, Jane excused herself to the ladies' room.

Max took that opportunity to thank the staff and sign autographs for those who asked for them. All the while he signed and thanked, he watched for Jane to return. When he'd settled back in his seat, he breathed a sigh.

He had to tell her about his connection to the NFL before they went much further in this discovery phase. It wouldn't be long before some photographer jumped out and snapped a picture and asked for a statement from him. He prayed she'd understand why he hadn't told her about his celebrity status and cut him some slack.

Hell, she trusted him. Telling her would let her down. Damn. He was going to regret not telling her sooner.

He'd planned to after their next date. The date where she met his group of friends. He had to admit, their dates had been a kind of proving ground. And she'd more than measured up to his expectations. The big question now was, would he measure up to hers?

Jane nearly died a thousand deaths of regret and remorse when the wait staff and the restaurant owner had addressed her as Ms. Gentry. Thankfully, they hadn't called her Angel, her stage name for her modeling career.

She'd struggled through dinner, barely tasting anything she ate and drinking a little too much wine. By the time the staff had taken away their plates, she had a headache and wished they could just leave. But she couldn't be rude to the staff after they'd been so kind.

A trip to the ladies' room was just what she needed to give her a chance to duck out and thank the owner, the maître d' and waiter for taking care of them that evening and remembering her from her last visit.

She'd stepped into the kitchen to thank the chef

as well and signed a few autographs for the men and women who worked so hard at Riomaggiore.

She'd hurried through her thanks and autographs to get back to the table with Max, praying he hadn't seen her talking with the staff or signing autographs. As they left the restaurant, Jane returned smiles with the staff but didn't say any more than she had to. She got outside as quickly as possible.

By that time, the sun had set, and a single streetlight lit the parking lot.

Max walked her to her car and made sure no one was in the back seat.

They were alone, for the moment. But how long that would last was in question. Other guests could come out at any time, possibly recognize her and ask for her autograph.

Jane couldn't completely relax until they were somewhere less public, and she didn't want to take him to her house in case he asked her how she'd come to own such an expensive place in one of the ritziest subdivisions in Austin.

She had to tell him who she was soon, why not now?

Jane turned her back to her car and took Max's hands in hers. "I enjoyed dinner with you."

"I did, too." He lifted her hands to his lips and brushed them with a feather-soft kiss. "I don't want the night to end, but my place is too far, and we drove separate vehicles. As much as I don't want our time together to end tonight, it's going to anyway." He kissed her fingers again. "Could you stand to see me again this weekend?" Max stared down into her eyes, his own brown ones shining in the glow from the streetlamp.

"And I don't want the night to end either," she said. "But, like you said, it must. And yes, please, I'd like to see you again." She frowned. "Wait. Seems like there's something on my calendar this weekend." Her eyes closed tightly, and her eyebrows drew together. Then she opened her eyes. "I have something Saturday night, but I'm free Friday."

"Good, because I was hoping for Friday night. Now that I think about it, I have a prior commitment scheduled for Saturday as well. One I can't get out of."

"Perfect. Friday it is."

"Oh, and wear something country," he said. "I'm taking you to a place my friends recommended that's close to my ranch, a place called the Ugly Stick Saloon. We're putting those dance lessons into practice."

Jane's eyes widened. She'd been to a lot of different places in her career but never a saloon. "We're going to a saloon?"

He nodded. "And I want you to meet a group of my friends."

Her cheeks heated. "You sure I'll fit in with them? I've never been to a saloon."

"You'll fit in perfectly. And if you don't, which I know you will, I won't care, because you fit in with me." He pulled her into his arms, tilted her chin up and covered her mouth with his.

She melted against his body and opened to him.

He swept his tongue past her teeth to claim hers in a long, sensuous caress.

Her body was soft against his hard planes. She was taller in her heels, but not too tall, and she liked that he didn't have to bend so far down to kiss her. They were more like partners in that respect than a man dominating a woman, and she liked that.

He leaned his forehead against hers. "I don't know if I can wait all the way until Friday," he said. "Tell me I can pick you up. It's a long drive out to the saloon, and you might want to stay at the ranch instead of driving all the back to Austin. It's up to you."

She tilted her head with a smile. "Are you sure?"

He nodded. "There are extra bedrooms in the house to choose from. No obligation, just making it convenient. We can stay longer at the saloon and not worry about driving all the way back."

She nodded. "I'll think about it. And yes, you can pick me up at my house. I live in a gated community, but I'll let the gate guard know you're coming."

"I'm glad to hear it. Living on your own can be dangerous. It's nice to know you go home to a gated community."

She nodded. "I'll text you the address."

He stared down at her for a long moment, and then bent to gently kiss her. "Now, go home before I'm tempted to stay here all night kissing you."

She chewed on her bottom lip for a moment, wondering if she was going to spook him by being too forward. But she wanted him so badly, she had to ask, "Do you want to come back to my place for a drink?"

He hesitated before answering.

Jane held her breath. Had she pushed too soon?

"I would," he said, "but I want you to know how much I care about you and how much I respect you. If I went with you now, I'd be too tempted to take advantage of you and go beyond kissing." He pulled her against him and held her long enough for her to understand the extent of his desire. The hard ridge of his cock beneath the zipper of his trousers pressed into her belly.

Her pulse quickened as she stared up at him. "I wouldn't have asked you to come to my house, if I didn't want you to go beyond kissing," she said, her voice husky.

He drew in a long breath and let it out. "Friday. I'm taking you dancing. What happens after that is up to you." He kissed her forehead, her eyelids one at a time and her mouth. "Still want to come?"

She nodded. "Even more so, now."

He set her away from him, opened her car door

and held it while she climbed in behind the wheel. "I'll see you Friday."

With every bit of control she could muster, she closed the door and started the engine.

She glanced in the rearview mirror as she drove out of the parking lot and out onto the street.

If all went according to plan, she'd be in his arms on Friday. On the dance floor and, hopefully, in his bed.

CHAPTER 12

Max showed up at the gate to Jane's subdivision Friday evening and waited for the gate guard to check his driver's license against the list of authorized guests before he let Max past the gate and gave him directions to Jane's house.

He was impressed by the homes in the community. They were upscale and appeared very expensive. If he'd chosen to live in Austin, it would have been in a neighborhood much like this. Private, carefully guarded and exclusive.

Max wondered how much a fashion merchandiser made to be able to afford to live in such a neighborhood. Each of the homes had to cost several million dollars, and they sat on large, beautifully landscaped lots of an acre or more.

When he pulled into the drive, Jane opened the door and came out before he stepped onto her paved walkway. She wore a blue denim skirt, a white tank top tucked into the skirt and white cowboy boots.

She carried a large leather purse, slung over her shoulder. Her hair was pulled back in a ponytail, low on the back of her neck, and what little makeup she wore enhanced her eyelashes and lips.

He met her halfway up the sidewalk to her front door and took her hands in his. "You look amazing."

She grinned. "You don't look bad yourself."

He'd worn a starched pair of blue jeans, white button-down shirt, cowboy boots and a cowboy hat. The hat was to help him hide his identity from anyone in the saloon who might recognize him, other than his friends, all of whom were coming and had been warned not to call him Moose or mention the NFL, his team or anything else about football.

Max glanced toward her house. "Do you need to lock up?"

"Already did." Her brow furrowed. "Did you want to go in?"

"Not unless you do."

She shook her head. "I have to confess, I've been watching videos on the internet. I think I have this two-step thing down. Only, I think it's probably harder with music and a real partner."

"You'll do fine. You did when we danced on our first date."

"You're too kind. I'll probably stomp on your toes until they're black and blue."

"I'll take my chances for the opportunity to hold you in my arms." He winked and held open the door to his truck. "Your chariot awaits."

With his assistance, she climbed up into the cab of the pickup and settled her purse on the floor.

Using the GPS, Max drove out of Austin, heading west, following the setting sun. They passed a town called Hellfire and another called Temptation before they came to what appeared to be a large tin shack in the middle of nowhere.

Max pulled into the parking lot where dozens of other trucks and SUVs were parked.

Even before he shut off the engine, he could hear the sound of country music pulsing through the corrugated tin walls.

Jane glanced his way, her eyes dancing. "This should be fun."

Max dropped down from the truck and rounded the hood to the passenger side.

Jane had the door open and was in the process of climbing out.

He helped her to the ground and nodded toward her purse. "Need that?"

She shook her head. "It can stay in the truck. I won't need it until later."

His pulse quickened. She'd brought what she'd need to stay the night at the ranch.

Max was tempted to say, *To hell with the Ugly Stick. Let's go to my place.*

But he'd promised to take her dancing, and he wanted to introduce her to his friends. He hadn't introduced a woman he was dating to his friends in a very long time.

His friends were his family, and he wanted them to know and love Jane.

They walked through the entrance and were greeted by the bouncer, a large, intimidating woman who looked like she chewed on nails for fun. "Can I see some ID?"

Jane laughed and pulled her driver's license out of her back pocket and showed it to the woman.

Max did the same.

The bouncer jerked her head toward the interior. "Welcome to the Ugly Stick Saloon."

It took a few moments standing just inside the saloon for his vision to adjust to the dim lighting and to find his friends seated at a table close to the dance floor.

Coop sat with his fiancée, Emma, and Gage had brought Fiona. Sean was on the dance floor with a cute brunette, and Tag was dancing Leslie around in a fast two-step. She was laughing but keeping up effortlessly.

"Gang's all here," Max said over the loud music.

With a hand at the small of Jane's back, Max guided her to the large table and made the introductions of the people seated.

"Guys, this is Jane Gentry." His chest puffed out.

He was so proud to be with her and to show her off to his friends. He went around the table, naming them. "Gage Tate is a good friend of mine from our college days at A&M. Actually, all the men here tonight are friends from my days at A&M," Max said. "Gage's lovely date is Fiona McKenzie."

The couple smiled and shook Jane's hand.

Max nodded toward Coop and his lady. "Coop Johnson and Emma Jacobs."

Coop rose to engulf Jane's hand in his larger one.

Emma rounded the table and hugged her. "It's so good to see Max with someone. He deserves to be happy, after all his hard work. I'm glad he's ranching fulltime. It's hard, but not as hard on his body as—"

"What would you like to drink?" Max interrupted, leaning close to Jane.

Emma's eyes rounded, and her cheeks flushed pink. "Sorry, didn't mean to keep a lady from her choice of libations." She hugged Jane once more and leaned back, studying her face. "I feel like I know you." Her eyes narrowed for a moment, and then she shrugged. "I'm sure it'll come to me later." She sat down beside Coop and rested her hand on his knee.

Max breathed a sigh.

Jane laughed shakily and turned to him. "I'll have a Miller Lite."

"Bottle or tap?" He lifted a hand to stop a strawberry-blond waitress passing by wearing a tank top and frayed jean shorts that barely covered her butt and bright red cowboy boots.

She smiled and nodded toward her full tray. "I'll be right back to take your order." After depositing mugs, bottles and snacks at another table, she returned.

"Hi, I'm Audrey Anderson Graywolf. I own this place. We're a little shorthanded, but we'll do the best we can. What can I get you?" Her grin spread across her face in a welcoming smile.

"Audrey, could you get us a couple of Miller Lites?" he asked.

She nodded. "I have it on tap or in the bottle."

"Tap is fine."

She nodded. "Anything else? Our barbeque sliders are on special tonight and meant to be shared."

"They're good," Coop added.

"Barbeque sliders it is," Max said with a smile. "Thank you."

Audrey left, her hair bouncing around her shoulders as she weaved her way between tables, calling out hello to customers entering the building.

Coop leaned forward. "Audrey's the best. She's really made this place come to life."

The music stopped between songs, and the band announced they would be taking a short break.

Sean left his dance partner at another table and sauntered over to join them. "This must be Jane," he said, holding out his hand. "I see why you talk so highly of her. She's gorgeous." He took Jane's hand in his and raised it to his lips to kiss the backs of her knuckles.

Max glared at him. "Hey."

Sean grinned and released her hand. "Nice to meet you Jane. Max has only good things to say about you."

She glanced up at him, her brow rising.

"Only good," he said, raising is hands in surrender. "I promise."

Tag and Leslie joined them.

"Jane, I'm so glad to finally meet you." Tag shook her hand, smiling. "Leslie speaks highly of you."

Jane shook his hand. "Leslie tells me you're a big proponent of BODS."

He nodded. "I am. So far, she's matched Coop and Gage with the loves of their lives. And look at you two…" Tag grinned. "I've never seen Moo—Max so discombobulated."

Jane glanced at Max, her brow twisting. "Max? Discombobulated?"

Her lips twitched, making Max want to kiss them. "He's just jealous I have a date and he doesn't." When Jane turned back to Tag, Max shot him a warning glare. He'd almost called him Moose.

Jane looked from Tag to Leslie. "Tag isn't your date?"

Leslie laughed and patted Tag's arm. "Oh, dear, no. We're just good friends. He's been one of my biggest supporters of BODS. I mean, look at him. He's gotten three out of his group of five men to give it a shot."

"Coop and Emma were first," Tag said. "They're getting married in a week."

Jane reached out and shook their hands again. "That's wonderful. Congratulations."

Max found himself envying Coop and Emma. They were already far enough into their relationship to tie the knot.

He wished he and Jane were there. The more he saw her, the more he wanted her to be in his life. Forever.

She hit all the qualifications on his bride test list. She was beautiful without all the makeup. Maybe she wasn't used to the outdoors as much as he was, but she was willing and had gotten dirty proving it. She was honest, kind and friendly. And she kissed like nobody's business. Though he'd told his friends that sex wasn't that important, he found himself longing to take her to bed and see if they fit as well there as they did in every other aspect.

Based on the bag she'd left in the truck, tonight might be his lucky night.

The band started up with "Cotton-Eyed Joe," breaking into Max's thoughts.

Sean beat him to the punch by leaning close to Jane and saying, "You look like a woman who needs to dance." He held out his hand. "Watch me make

Max jealous." He winked at her and grinned at Max. "Mind if I borrow Ms. Jane?"

"Actually, I do," Max said.

"Good. Then I've accomplished my mission." He pulled Jane's hand through his elbow and out onto the dance floor.

Max growled.

"She isn't into Sean," Tag reminded him.

"Yeah, but he's good with the ladies," Max pointed out.

Already, Sean had Jane dancing around the floor to the song and shouting bullshit with the rest of the crowd.

Max held back from marching out onto the floor and punching his friend's lights out. Had the song been good for the two-step, he might have done it.

He wanted to be Jane's dance partner when she did the two-step for the first time in a dance hall.

The song ended, and the dancers all laughed and clapped.

Max moved toward Sean and Jane as they headed back to the table.

Before they reached him, a large, swaying cowboy grabbed Jane's elbow and jerked her toward the dance floor.

At first, Sean didn't see him. He was too busy flirting with a woman he'd danced with earlier.

Meanwhile, the big, burly cowboy dragged Jane in amongst the dancers.

Her brow furrowed, and she glanced around the room as if searching for...

Their gazes met, and she mouthed the word, *Help.*

Max picked up speed and charged into the dancers, bumping them aside to get to Jane.

The cowboy had his back to him when Max politely tapped his shoulder.

"Shove off," the cowboy said, his voice slurring.

"That's my girl you've got there," Max said, his voice stern.

"She's mine now," the cowboy said and pulled Jane closer.

"Perhaps you'd better ask her who she prefers," Max said, standing so close the cowboy had to stop or plow into him.

"You heard me, shove off!" The cowboy dropped his hold on Jane and swung at Max.

Max ducked the swing and used the cowboy's momentum to spin him around. He grabbed his arm and yanked it up behind his back.

Audrey and the female bouncer were there immediately.

"Greta Sue, take Billy Ray's arm, while I call for the deputy sheriff to help him find his way home."

"I've got him," Greta Sue said in a disturbingly deep voice.

Max yielded his hold on Billy Ray and kept his body between the cowboy and Jane until Greta Sue guided the man out of the building, pushing his arm up between his shoulder blades until the man was staggering on his tiptoes to relieve the pain.

A hand touched Max's shoulder. He turned to face Jane. "Sorry for that."

"Why? You saved me from getting my toes stomped. And you probably saved that man's life. If he'd driven himself home, he might have run off the road, or killed someone else." She held open her arms. "I thought we were going to two-step. Is this a song we can dance to?"

"I don't care if it is or isn't. I want you in my arms." He pulled her close and held her for a moment, just swaying. "You smell good, like honey-suckle in the spring."

She laughed and smiled up at him. "And you smell like manly heaven."

His lips twisted. "I'll take that as a compliment. I think."

She nodded. "You should."

"I wanted to be the first man to lead you out on the dance floor in a two-step."

"This might be your lucky day. I'm not sure what dance moves Billy Ray was using, but it wasn't a two-step." She took her hand in his and guided his other one to the middle of her back.

Max started dancing, murmuring, "Quick, quick, slooow, slooow." When she had the steps down, he asked, "Got it?"

She nodded. "Got it."

He circled the dance floor with Jane in his arms, loving every minute of being with her. He could see them dancing the two-step with gray hair, years down the road. She'd look amazing with gray hair. Never had he imagined himself with anyone, drifting into old age.

The music slowed to a tune perfect for belly-rubbing and swaying in place. Max gathered Jane close and rested his chin against her temple.

She wrapped her arms around his neck and pulled his face down close to hers. "I could stay like this forever," she whispered.

"Me, too." Then he kissed her, and she kissed him back.

The music ended, and the band announced another break, but Max and Jane continued to sway and kiss.

When he finally came up for air, the crowd in the bar burst into applause, wolf-calling and whistling.

Jane blushed.

"Did you want to stay and dance?" he asked. "I have wine and food at the ranch, if you'd rather go somewhere quieter."

She nodded. "I would. But what about your friends?"

Max nodded toward their table. "Coop and Emma left while we were dancing. Same with Gabe and Fiona. Tag and Leslie seem to be enjoying dancing with each other, and Sean's found another lady to entertain him. They won't miss us."

"If you're sure, I'd like to go." She touched his chest. "I enjoyed dancing with you."

"And you're a quick learner. We make a good team." He hoped they could become a permanent team. "As they said, Coop and Emma are getting married in a week. How are you with attending a wedding?"

"I've been to one or two." Her lips twitched. "I was well-behaved at both, if that's what you're asking."

He chuckled. "I'd be honored if you'd be my plus one."

"I'd love to go."

"Do you need to look at your calendar first?"

"I'm free. My last formal commitment from my previous career is tomorrow night."

"I'm booked tomorrow night as well. If I hadn't had that one engagement, I'd have loved seeing you again."

"Again?" She slipped her hand into his. "We haven't parted yet."

He smiled. "Right. Shall we slip out while no one is looking?"

She nodded. "That would eliminate the need for long goodbyes."

"True." He cupped her elbow and walked her toward the exit.

Greta Sue held out her hand toward Max. "Thank

you for helping with Billy Ray, Mr. Smithson. I love watching you on Monday nights." She grinned and pumped his hand.

"Uh, thanks," Max said, his cheeks hot as he shook Greta Sue's hand and hurried Jane outside into the clear night air.

"What did she mean she loved to watch you on Monday nights?" Jane asked.

"She must have mistaken me for someone else. I didn't want to argue with her." He held the passenger door for her to climb up into the truck.

Her skirt hiked up, showing a significant amount of thigh.

Max's groin tightened as he spotted the bag on the floorboard.

If he was not mistaken, she'd come prepared to stay the night. His actions would determine whether or not she actually made the decision to stay.

He wished she'd come with a playbook. Having been a quarterback, he'd made decisions on the fly, based on the movements of players on the field.

With Jane, Max was playing a position he wasn't familiar with and winging it all the way.

"That was fun," she said, as he climbed into the driver's seat. "I never knew two-stepping was so easy."

"You learned quickly. Next time, we'll stay long enough to learn some of the line dances. I think you'll enjoy those, as well."

She smiled and sat back in her seat. "I'd like that." She turned toward him, her smile widening. "But right now, I'd rather go somewhere quiet, where we can hear ourselves think."

"I'd tell you it was quiet out at the ranch, but the cicadas are in full force, singing up a storm. They can be as loud as the band at the Ugly Stick."

"But it's a different kind of noise. I don't feel like I have to shout over them to carry on a conversation."

"True," Max said. He hoped they wouldn't be carrying on lengthy conversations. Not when he'd rather be kissing every inch of her naked body.

By the time he drove through the gates of his ranch, he was ready to strip, throw her over his shoulder, carry her up to his bedroom and make sweet love to every inch of her beautiful body.

As he shifted into park in front of the house, he drew in a deep breath and let it out before he climbed down. Rounding the front of the truck, he opened the passenger door, gripped Jane around the waist, lifted her out of her seat and let her slowly slide down his body until her feet touched the ground.

She wrapped her arms around his neck. When their mouths collided, it felt like spontaneous combustion ignited. Adrenaline raced through his veins, and his desire shot straight to his cock

He lifted his lips from hers and rested his forehead against hers.

"I've wanted to hold you like that all night," she said, echoing his thoughts.

"Babe, I haven't thought of anything else." Max kissed her again, his hand sliding down her back to cup her ass. He pressed her against the ridge of his cock, nudging his hardness against her soft belly.

He groaned and leaned back. "Tell me to stop now. I'm not so certain I'll be able to stop later."

She shook her head and cupped his cheek. "Don't stop. I haven't thought of much else since you invited me to stay at the ranch. I can't tell you how many times I packed and repacked my bag." She laughed. "I'm not certain what's in it at this point. And I really don't care. As long as I can spend an evening with you. I'm not asking you to marry me, or to promise to commit the rest of your life to making me happy." She leaned up on her toes. "And I know I'm babbling. So, kiss me."

Max gave her a brief kiss, and then bent and scooped her and her bag up in his arms, carrying her into the house, up the staircase and into the master bedroom before he set her back on her feet. This was what he'd wanted since their first date. And finally, she was there with him. Now, if only he could keep her there forever.

CHAPTER 13

JANE LAUGHED and clung to him. "You didn't even breathe hard coming up the steps."

"It's the adrenaline. Perhaps, I read too much into your request for me to kiss you, but I hope I didn't."

She looked up at him, her cheeks heating along with the rest of her body in response to the desire shining from his eyes. "You're not reading too much into my request. I want more than a kiss." To prove it, she reached for the top button of his shirt and flicked it open.

Max closed his eyes, a growl rumbling in his chest. "Too slow," he murmured.

"Is that so?" she asked, a smile tugging at her lips. She increased the pace, flipping open the buttons and yanking loose his shirttail from the waistband of his trousers.

He shrugged out of the garment and flung it across the room.

Then he spun her around and slid the zipper of her skirt down.

Jane shivered, her body on fire. When the skirt caught on her hips, she shoved it the rest of the way down her thighs and kicked free of it.

Then she turned to face him, wearing only her bra, a pair of thong panties that did nothing to cover her ass and the cowboy boots. And she'd never felt sexier.

His gaze raked over her, his desire warm in his eyes. "You're amazing."

"You're overdressed," she said and reached for the button on his jeans, wrestling it free with a flick of her wrist.

As the denim fell down around his ankles, he toed off his boots and stepped free of the jeans, revealing he'd gone commando beneath.

"Now, you're overdressed," he said, standing in front of her completely naked and absolutely magnificent in his male glory. His cock jutted out straight and hard.

Jane's core coiled and heated. She reached behind her and unhooked the catches on her bra, letting the straps slip down her arms. Her breasts bounced free. The coolness of the airconditioned room and the way he was looking at her made her nipples tighten into hard little beads.

When she raised her hands to her hips and the elastic of her panties, he stopped her with both hands covering hers.

"Let me," he said, his voice deep and rough.

She gave him a slight nod and lifted her hands, surrendering to whatever he had in mind.

He backed her up until she bumped into the king-size bed and sat on the edge. Then he leaned over her until she lay back on the mattress and wrapped her arms around his neck.

Max kissed her, driving his tongue between her teeth to claim hers in a long, soul-defining caress that left her breathless and longing for more.

Leaving her mouth, he trailed his lips across her chin and down her neck to the pulse beating so fast at the base of her throat.

Her body was on fire, the flames threatening to consume her.

Max traveled down her body, stopping to capture one of her breasts in his palm while he took the other into his mouth, sucking hard, and then teasing the nipple with flicks of his tongue and gentle nips.

Jane moaned and arched off the mattress, wanting him to take more, to completely devour her, one bite, one flick and one touch at a time.

"Max," she whispered.

"Yes, Jane," he said, his breath blowing warm air over her damp nipple, sending shivers across her nerve endings.

"Take me. Come inside me," she said on a strangled sigh. "I want you."

"I will," he promised. "When you're ready."

"Oh, sweet heaven, I'm ready," she cried. Her body ached with her desire and her core heated, her channel slick with her need.

Still, he took his sweet time caressing every inch of her with his mouth and tongue. Leaving her breasts, he trailed kisses down her torso, paying homage to each rib and the indention of her belly-button. He didn't stop until he reached the edge of her panties.

Hooking his fingers into the elastic, he dragged them down, exposing the tuft of curls covering her sex. Pulling her panties further down her legs, he licked her inner thighs, causing another moan to escape her lips.

"Hurry," she begged. "I can't wait much longer."

His chuckle warmed the skin over her calves and finally, he tugged her panties past her ankles, freeing her to spread her legs and open herself to him.

When she tried to kick off her boots, he laid his hands over her feet. "No," he said. "Leave them on."

Inch by inch, he worked his way up her legs, trailing his fingers up the inside of her thighs to her wet center. He slipped two digits into her channel and swirled in the juices.

Jane closed her eyes, writhing against the comforter, lost in the haze of an overpowering lust.

"Please," she moaned. "Don't make me wait."

"Soon," he said. "First, I want you to come apart."

"I am."

"No, you haven't," he said. "Not yet."

Max dipped the fingers of one hand into her and parted her folds with the other. Then he bent to flick the strip of flesh between.

Jane pulled up her knees and dug her heels into the mattress, rising up to meet Max's mouth.

He swirled his tongue over her clit, again and again.

Jane catapulted over the edge, rocketing into the stratosphere on an orgasm that shook her body to its very core.

She held still for a long moment and then pumped her hips, urging him to continue teasing her senses until she'd spent the fiery sensations and lay back against the mattress, breathing hard as if she'd run a marathon.

Then she was pulling on his hair, dragging him up her body until his cock nudged her entrance.

He paused, leaned to the side and dug into the drawer beside the bed. Seconds later, he held up a small packet, tore it open and leaned back to roll the condom over his engorged staff.

"I'm...glad...someone can still think," Jane said, her voice broken, her breathing coming in strangled gasps.

He bent to kiss her, his mouth tasting of her sex.

With his sheathed erection poised at her entrance, he kissed her again and slid inside her at the same time.

Jane dug her feet into the mattress and rose to meet his thrust, taking him all the way inside her.

Her channel clenched around his wide girth.

He remained buried inside her long enough for her to adjust to his size. When she thought she couldn't take more, he moved out of her.

She gripped his butt cheeks and pulled him back in.

He settled into a slow steady rhythm, increasing the speed incrementally until he was pumping in and out of her like a piston.

Jane's fingers dug into his ass, her thoughts scrambled, her focus on the man making love to her like they might not have tomorrow.

Sensations built to a roiling crescendo, and she came again.

At that exact moment, Max thrust one last time and remained deep inside her, his cock pulsing with his release, his body rigid.

When at last his muscles relaxed, he collapsed on top of her and rolled them both to the side. His breath was ragged, and his hand curled tightly against her hip.

She lay with her cheek against his chest, listening to the rapid beat of his heart and reveling in what had just happened between them.

She'd brought him to this point. He'd lost himself in her. It gave her a feeling of power and awe.

They lay for a long time, connected so intimately. Jane didn't want to move, didn't want to leave, but knew she would have to all too soon.

"MAX," a soft voice called to him.

He blinked his eyes open and stared up into violet eyes so beautiful he smiled. "Hey, gorgeous."

"Hey," Jane said. "I'd love to stay in bed with you all day, but I need to get home. I have a commitment I need to be at tonight, and I need to get ready."

He pulled her into his arms and held her against his chest for a long moment. "I'll take you home on one condition."

She laughed, her naked body feeling so right against his. "And that is?"

"That we do this again...soon."

"Deal," she said.

His dick hardened. "How soon do you have to leave?"

"Within the next thirty minutes." She leaned up on his chest and stared down into his eyes. "Do you realize it's past noon?"

"If you hadn't kept me up all night, we wouldn't have slept in so late." He winked at her.

"I didn't know a man could come so many times

in one night." She wiggled against him, her soft abdomen doing sexy things to his hard-on.

"Thirty minutes is a long time," he said. "Unless you feel compelled to eat before we leave."

"It's a good thing we had a snack at four this morning. I'm not starving…" she said, "for food." Jane kissed his neck and worked her way down his body, kissing his neck, collarbone and lower to take a dark nipple between her teeth and roll it gently.

She didn't pause long before she continued her trajectory south to the jutting evidence of his desire.

Grasping him in her hand, she wrapped her fingers around his shaft and bent to take him into her mouth.

Max groaned and thrust upward.

She took all of him, sliding her warm wet tongue around him.

He pumped in and out of her mouth, until he was so close to his release he struggled for control.

Pulling free, he flipped her onto her back, located and applied protection, and then drove into her in one, swift thrust that buried him all the way inside her.

She wrapped her legs around his middle and dug her boot heels into his buttocks, holding him inside her until he'd spent his release.

When he finally came back to earth, he kissed her long and hard, and then gathered her in his arms and carried her into the shower.

Together, they washed each other's bodies and toweled the other dry.

While Jane dressed in jeans and a white tank top, Max pulled on jeans, a black T-shirt and his boots.

They kissed again and walked out to his truck in silence, the glow of their lovemaking so fresh they didn't need to talk and probably couldn't.

The drive back to Austin was accomplished in relative silence, both lost in their own thoughts.

When Max pulled up to the gate of Jane's community, Jane leaned over him, asking the gate guard to let them through.

At her house, she waited for him to open her door for her and help her down from the truck. She clung to him for a long moment.

"When will I see you again?" he asked.

"Sunday?" Jane suggested.

"Sunday," he said, but didn't move away. "I don't want to leave you."

"Mmm. I don't want you to," she said, laying her cheek against his chest. "If I didn't have this commitment, I wouldn't."

"Same." He tilted up her chin and gave her a gentle kiss. "Sunday."

She nodded, stepped out of his arms and walked into her house, closing the door behind her.

Max climbed into his truck, tempted to call his agent and tell him he was sick and couldn't make the engagement that night. Now that he'd found Jane, he didn't want to be away from her. Ever.

But he didn't back out of obligations. Especially ones as important as tonight's.

Max sucked in a deep breath, let it out and climbed into his pickup. Then he headed for his agent's office where he'd pick up what he needed for that evening. He'd hole up at Tag's place until the time he had to show up before he went on stage.

If he didn't believe in what they were doing, he wouldn't have agreed to be a part of the whole production. But it was important, and he'd be there.

Afterward, he'd call Jane and see if they could meet that night, instead of waiting until Sunday. He wasn't sure he could wait that long.

At his agent's office, he was greeted with a duffle bag full of stuff that would be auctioned off that night. The only catch was that he had to wear it in order to display it to the potential bidders.

Once he had the items, he left his agent with a handshake and a promise to meet him for coffee in the near future.

With a couple of hours to spare, Max tossed the duffle into the back seat of the truck, locked it and went for a walk down the block.

Hadn't he seen a jewelry store near his agent's office? He'd like to get something nice for Jane.

Max found the jewelry store and entered, feeling like a bull in a china shop. Everything was delicate and shiny. Though all the bling was pretty, it wasn't something Max was interested in. Though he wasn't enthralled with the items displayed, he could picture some of them on Jane, and he looked closer.

Would she wear a diamond bracelet? He paused in front of glass display cabinet with shiny bracelets. His gaze moved to the next cabinet filled with diamond earrings. What about those? Would she wear them? Would she think he was a jerk for buying her jewelry after having sex?

He shoved a hand through his hair and moved to the next display case.

"Are you looking for something in particular?" the saleswoman asked.

"I don't know."

"Who are you buying for?" she asked.

"A very special woman," he said.

"Your mother or grandmother?" she asked.

"No. A..." he hesitated and ended up saying, "friend."

The woman gave him a gentle smile. "Only a friend?" she asked. "Do you love her?"

Max's pulse sped, and his face flushed with heat. Did he love Jane? "I've only known her for a week," he admitted to the stranger.

She shook her head. "When it's the right one, you just know. I knew the moment I met my husband." The women held up her hand with her wedding ring. "We've been married for thirty-five years. I still love him as much as the day I married him, if not more. I knew he was the one I wanted to grow old with." She snorted softly. "And danged if we aren't growing old together."

Max smiled at the woman. "Congratulations. Not many marriages last that long."

"Not many people work at them to keep them going. Marriage isn't easy, but it's wonderful if you marry the right person."

"How do you know when it's the right person?" he asked.

"Does she make you want to be with her twenty-four-seven?"

He nodded.

"Do you feel like half of you is missing when you're not with her?" the woman asked.

Max nodded. "Yes. I feel like I can't remember how to breathe."

She smiled. "Sir, you're in love."

He pressed a hand to his tight chest. "I am?"

"Sounds like it to me. Otherwise, why did you come into the store?" She raised both eyebrows and tipped her head. "You passed the bracelets and earrings. What you're really looking for is one of these."

She pulled out a tray of diamond engagement rings.

He held up his hands and backed away a step or

two. "I'm not ready to ask her to marry me. I told you, we only met a week ago."

She gave him a knowing smile. "A week, a month, a year. If you know…you know."

Max walked out of the store having spent over twenty grand, shaking his head, wondering what had just happened. Had he lost his senses? He couldn't possibly contemplate doing what he was going to do, following the event that night.

He had until he saw Jane again to change his mind. The woman in the store assured him that if things didn't go according to plan, he could return his purchase within a week and get a full refund.

Max didn't give a rat's ass about the return. He only cared that he didn't spook Jane by jumping the gun. Even if he was absolutely certain he wanted Jane in his life forever, Jane might not be as keen on forever as he was.

Was he insane?

Yes.

Was that fact going to stop him?

Hell, no.

CHAPTER 14

Jane stood on the right side of the stage, while the ladies who'd designed the bodysuit adjusted the ostrich feather wings attached to her back.

Her agent parked himself beside her, talking nonstop in an attempt to convince her that she was making a huge mistake, getting out of the modeling business so soon.

"Layne," Jane finally cut him off. "My decision is not up for discussion. I have more money than I know what to do with, I have businesses that continue to make more, and I want a life before I'm too old to enjoy it."

"You can have that life. I know lots of models who marry, have children and get right back out on that runway."

"That's just it, I don't want to be that model. I

want to be Plain Jane, soccer mom, and remote-access businesswoman. Maybe on a ranch out in the middle of nowhere."

She smiled at the image she had of standing on the porch, staring out at the pastures of the ranch where Max worked. They might have to have a ranch of their own, if his boss drew the line at a family filling his house.

Assuming Max was as interested in her as she was in him. And assuming he had marriage and family in mind.

After last night, Jane knew. Max was the man for her. He'd taken his time to get to know her without rushing her into sex. Hell, if anything, she had rushed him into making love to her. Her lips quirked.

"What are you smiling about?" Layne asked.

"Nothing you would understand," she said. "I'm only here tonight for the children." Jane adjusted the straps on the beautiful gown that had been donated by an upscale designer out of New York. The guests in the audience had money. Lots of it. The dress should bring a tidy sum at auction.

All she had to do was walk the runway in it, displaying it to its full potential, and then wait while the event organizers auctioned it off to the highest bidder. Once the final bid was recorded, she'd walk off the runway for the last time, strip out of the dress and put on her own dress, make an appearance in front of the media and get the hell out of the lime-light and on her way back home.

She glanced at her cellphone, sitting on the table beside her. How she wished Max would call and tell her he'd had a great time last night.

More than anything, she wanted to tell him she was falling in love with him and wanted to spend the rest of her life with him. He was everything she'd ever wanted in a husband: kind, hard-working, protective and honest.

Being a celebrity had its drawbacks. Jane never knew when someone was telling her the truth or blowing smoke up her skirts, just to get her to agree to some scheme or another.

With Max, she felt like she could let her guard down. She didn't have to be anyone but herself, and she didn't have to worry that he was taking advantage of her. He didn't know what she was worth in dollars. She could be as poor as a church mouse and he didn't seem to care.

And Jane didn't care that he was only a ranch hand. He must have had to work overtime, and then some, to afford to take her out to the Riomaggiore restaurant.

She grimaced, wishing she'd gotten ahead of the bill and paid it down so that Max wouldn't have had to spend so much of his hard-earned cash just trying to impress her.

Perhaps it was time to tell him everything about her life. Hopefully, he wouldn't be intimidated that she made so much money or suddenly get greedy and want the money more than her.

Jane straightened and stared at her reflection in the mirror. Her makeup covered her face entirely, transforming her from Plain Jane Gentry to her stage name of Angel Gentry.

Her blond curls had been slicked back from her forehead and straightened to fall down to her waist behind her. She wasn't the makeup-free woman who'd ridden ATVs and fallen in the mud out at the ranch with Max. She wasn't the Jane she wanted to be. "Layne, this is my last runway gig. I'm retiring after this. I'm one hundred percent sure."

Layne looked over her shoulder at her reflection and nodded. "Okay. I'll have to come up with another way to put my daughter through college."

Jane shook her head. "Don't lay the guilt trip on me, Layne. You've made more than enough off me alone to put a dozen children through college."

He grinned. "Yes, but you were my most lucrative client to date."

"You'll find another model who'll be even more impressive." She turned and gave the man an air kiss on his cheek to avoid smearing her makeup or leaving a print. "You know I'll always love you and your wife. Now, tell me who comes after me?"

His eyes lit up. "The Texas Ramblers' star quarterback. They're auctioning off his jersey, pads and helmet. I'd give my first born for that prize, if my wife would let me."

"That's football, right?" she asked.

Layne rolled his eyes. "Woman, don't you watch sports at all?"

She shook her head. "I haven't had time. But I plan to remedy that. I want to know what all the fuss is about the game. I mean, who's this star quarter-back, and why is he so popular that they'd auction off his jersey?"

"He's only the best quarterback in the NFL. The Ramblers are going to hurt now that he's retiring."

"See? He probably wants a life, too. Why shouldn't I?" She wondered if Max knew of the football player, and if he watched the game. She'd learn to love foot-ball if Max loved it. Anything to spend time with him and be a part of his life.

The event MC announced the next item on the auction list. "Displayed by the incomparable, world-renowned supermodel, Angel Gentry."

"You're on," Layne said. "Make it count, it's your last hurrah."

She nodded, squared her shoulders, pasted on her model poker face and stepped out onto the stage, passing a famous male movie star, wearing the suit he'd starred in during the filming of his last action-adventure movie.

She gave him a barely perceptible nod and walked

to the end of the stage, relishing the moment, knowing it would be her last stroll down the runway. After this, she could truly begin the next chapter of her life.

Joy and hope warred with her nerves. She'd been modeling for so long she wasn't sure she'd know what to do with herself when it was all over.

Marriage and children, she told herself. *Keep your eye on the prize, and it will happen.*

MAX STOOD on the left side of the stage, queuing up to be next to strut his stuff for the children's charity auction. In his full set of pads, jersey and helmet, he was geared up to hit the football field. It felt at once normal and surreal.

He hadn't worn his gear since his last Super Bowl. Tonight, he wore the championship ring and had donated his jersey, pads and helmet to the auction, hoping to bring lots of money for the children's hospital.

"You all right?" Tag asked as he stood beside him in the wings.

"A little warm, but, yeah, all right." Max turned to look through the mask at his friend. "I'm ready for this to be over."

Tag grinned. "What? You have better plans on a Saturday night?"

"No. But I hope to," he said.

Tag gave him the side-eye. "Would they have anything to do with Jane?"

Max nodded. "Everything to do with Jane. If I find her after this circus, I'm going to ask her to marry me."

Tag's eyes widened. "You're kidding, right?"

Max's brow dipped at the center. "Why do you say it like that? Do you think it's too soon?"

"You've only known each other a week," Tag argued.

"But when you know she's the one for you…you know, right?" Max's heart thundered at the thought of popping the question. What if it was too soon? What if she wasn't sure yet. Would asking her after only a week send her running in the opposite direction?

Damn. He wanted her so badly, the ring he'd purchased seemed to be burning a hole into his subconscious. If he could see her later that night, he'd get a feel for where she was at in their relationship.

Oh, hell, who was he kidding? He would ask her, no matter what her answer entailed. If she didn't say yes, immediately, he'd ask her to at least think about it before she gave him her response.

"Who am I following?" he asked Tag.

"You're after the supermodel, Angel Gentry. She's out there now." Tag pulled aside the curtain enough he could look out at the runway. "Wow, she's gorgeous."

Max didn't care about the supermodel. He loved Jane and was going to ask her to marry him as soon as he could get her alone.

The event coordinator hurried up to Max, carrying a clipboard and a harried expression on her face. "Mr. Smithson, you need to get out on stage."

"What am I supposed to do?"

"You'll walk out to the end of the runway. Stand there for a long moment, letting the audience see what they're bidding on, and then turn and walk slowly back to this side of the stage." She gave him a shaky smile. "That's all."

He nodded and stepped out onto the stage. With the lights shining in his eyes, and the grill on his mask blocking some of his vision, Max found it difficult to see.

When he reached the middle of the stage, he paused, and pulled the helmet off his head. He figured, carrying it would be good enough. That way he didn't walk off the end of the runway and crash into the crowd. A light-weight model was an easier catch than a two-hundred-and-thirty-pound football player in full gear.

Ah, he could see just in time to watch the super-model swaying down the runway toward him.

He frowned. Wasn't she the one who'd fallen into

his arms in Vegas? The one with the violet eyes so much like Jane's.

His brows dipped.

The model slowed as she approached him. Her poker face slipped into a narrow-eyed frown as she came closer. And her feet faltered in those ridiculously high heels.

Why did women do that to themselves?

The MC keyed the microphone and announced, "Please welcome Moose Smithson, NFL star quarterback for the Texas Ramblers, wearing his full football gear, jersey and helmet to be auctioned here tonight."

As Angel came abreast of him, she stopped, her eyes widening. "Max?"

Max frowned, staring at the woman so covered in makeup, he had no idea who she was, until she'd spoken his name.

"Max? Is that you?" she said.

"Jane?" His pulse leaped, and he reached for the woman, not really believing what he was seeing. "Jane? Is that you?"

"What the hell?" she said and leaned back, her gaze going over him from head to toe. "I thought you were just a rancher."

As the truth of Jane's appearance sank in, Max stepped backward. "I thought you were just a woman, not a supermodel. Why didn't you tell me?"

"Why didn't you tell me you were some superstar

football player?" Her eyes filled with tears. "I thought you were an honest man, someone I could trust."

"And I thought you were just a woman, looking for a partner in your life, not...this." He waved a hand toward her face, her clothes, those horrible heels.

Jane snorted. "So, you're a fake, and I'm a phony. I guess that makes us even. I guess that's it. You feed lies into a program, and it'll give you whatever you asked for. That's too bad. Leslie had high hopes for BODS." Jane held out her hand. "It was nice while it lasted, Mr. Smithson."

He took her hand in his, anger burning hot in his veins. "Yeah. I guess you got a good laugh out of my rancher routine."

"And you must have loved seeing me covered in mud." She shook her head. "Have a wonderful life playing football."

"And you have a wonderful life walking the runway." He added, "I hope you don't break your neck the next time you fall off your heels in Vegas."

"I'm sure there will be someone there to catch me. There always is." She turned and hurried off the stage.

Max walked to the end of the runway, barely able to focus on the auction when his heart was breaking into pieces.

She'd been lying to him the entire week, telling him she was into fashion merchandizing.

Well, hadn't he lied about being a rancher after a career in sports management?

The auction went on around him, while his thoughts roiled around the Jane he'd grown to love and Angel, her supermodel antithesis.

What right did he have to be angry with her when he was equally at fault? He should have been up front with her all along.

But he'd been afraid she wouldn't love him for who he wanted to be, not who he'd been as an NFL football player.

Holy hell, she had probably been afraid he wouldn't love her for who she wanted to be rather than who she had been as a supermodel.

"Sold!" the auctioneer shouted. The crowd erupted into applause, Max's cue to leave the stage.

He hurried down the runway passing an actress who'd starred in a sci-fi series. He gave her a brief nod and made a sharp right turn in the direction Jane had left the stage. Once behind the curtain, he shoved his helmet into the event coordinator's arms. "Where is she?" he demanded.

The woman looked up from her clipboard. "Where's who?"

"Jane—Angel Gentry. Where is she?" Max wanted to reach out and shake the information out of the coordinator.

"She's probably in the dressing room, getting out of the gown she wore. Why?"

"Because, I love her, and I'll be damned if she walks out of my life before I have a chance to convince her to marry me."

The woman smiled and shook her head. "Ah, young love." She shot a glance at her clipboard and looked up again with a smile. "Room eleven. And good luck!"

Still wearing his pads and jersey, Max plowed through the celebrities lined up for their turn on stage and raced to the rear of the theater where the dressing rooms lined the wall.

"Moose!" a voice called out.

Max turned to find Tag running to catch up to him. "What happened? Why did you run off the wrong side of the stage?"

"Angel is Jane," he said, continuing past one dressing room door after another, searching for door number eleven.

When he came to his dressing room, he ducked in, grabbed the little box out of the pocket of his trousers and curled it into his hand before running back out into the hallway.

Tag caught up and ran alongside him, "I don't understand. What do you mean?"

"Supermodel Angel Gentry is also the woman I've been dating, Jane Gentry. I don't know why I didn't see it. It was there in her eyes. No two women could possibly have that shade of violet. I should have known."

"So, she'd not the Plain Jane you advertised for. Why are you so bent on finding her?" Tag asked.

"I have to find her. She has to know."

"What does she have to know?"

Eleven. The door was directly in front of him. He didn't hesitate. Raising his hand he knocked.

"Go away," Jane's voice sounded behind the panel.

Max tried the door, but it was locked. "I'm not going away until you talk to me."

"I don't want to talk to you," she said.

"I think she's crying," Tag whispered.

Max's heart twisted hard in his chest. "Damn it, Jane, open the door."

"No. We have nothing left to say." Her voice was louder, less muffled, as if she'd moved closer to the door.

Max leaned his forehead against the door, no mean feat when he was still bulked-out in pads. "I know why you didn't tell me. It's the same reason I didn't tell you. It doesn't matter."

"Yes, it does. We'll never be able to trust each other."

"We will. Because people who learn to love each other, learn to trust one another."

"No, they don't."

"Jane, open the door. I need to see your violet eyes. I need to tell you to your face, not through this door, that I love you. I think I fell in love with your eyes the first time I saw you in Vegas. But it was the

Jane who slid in the mud that I've fallen head over heels for."

"But we've only known each other for a week."

"It doesn't matter. When you know, you know."

"Now that you know I'm Angel, how do I know you don't love Angel better than Jane?"

"Because Angel isn't the woman I made love to last night. Jane is the woman who rode ATVs with me on the ranch. Jane is the one I love and want to be a part of my life forever."

"I can't continue to be hounded by paparazzi. I'm done with being in the public eye."

"Me, too. I retired as of my last game. I'm a full-time rancher now."

"You are?" she asked, her voice soft behind the panel.

"I am." He rested the hand holding the box against the door. "Jane, open the door."

A long pause stretched between them. Max was about to go find someone to unlock the door so that he could get to Jane, hold her in his arms and tell her to her face that he'd fallen madly in love with her.

A soft click sounded, and the doorknob turned.

"Uh, I'll leave you two alone," Tag said and backed away before the door opened and Jane peered out at him, her makeup smeared by the tracks of her tears.

She'd changed out of her dress into a thin, oriental robe and stood in her bare feet.

"Why did you lie to me?" she asked, more tears streaming down her face.

"I wanted to find someone real, someone who would be satisfied to live on a ranch, raise children and make a home with me. I'd had enough of the women who were only after me because I was a famous football player and had a lot of money." He reached for her hands. "Why did you lie to me?"

"I wanted all those things, too. I want to hold my babies in my arms before I'm too old to have them. I wanted a man to love me for Jane, not because I've been Angel for the past sixteen years. I need to be loved for me." Tears made trails through the mascara smeared on her cheeks.

Max shook his head, pulled the handkerchief from his pocket and dabbed at her tears. "I fell in love with *you*, not Angel."

Her lower lip trembled. "Now that you know I'm Angel as well, you haven't changed your mind?"

He shook his head and raised the hand holding the little box. "I was going to call you after this event. If you'd have let me, I'd have come to your house."

"I would have let you in," she said, her voice softening.

He smiled and brushed his thumb across her cheek, wiping away another tear. "It might have been too soon, and you will probably tell me no, but I couldn't wait another minute to tell you."

She looked up into his eyes. "Tell me what?" she asked, her voice barely a whisper.

He knelt on one knee. "To tell you how much I love you and want you to be a part of my life, forever." He opened the little box, displaying the beautiful diamond engagement ring he'd chosen because he thought it would look perfect for her hand.

"Jane Gentry, will you make me the happiest man on earth and marry me?"

She sniffed. "What about Angel? Will it bother you that I'll be stalked by the paparazzi and asked to make guest appearances at charity events like this?"

"Jane Gentry, will you and your alter ego, Angel, marry me and make me the happiest man on earth? I promise I'll love all of you and do my very best to give you the babies you have your heart set on and the home to raise them in."

More tears trailed down her cheeks.

"Oh, sweetheart, if you don't want to marry me, tell me," he said. "I hate to see you cry."

She laughed, choking on a sob. "These are happy tears."

"I'm sorry I lied to you about being just a rancher. But I am just a rancher now. I'm not going to play football again. I want to keep what's left of my body healthy enough to watch my children and grandchildren grow." He held the ring box a little higher. "If you don't like the ring, we can trade it for one that you like better. Anything. Just say yes."

Jane dropped to her knees in front of him and flung her arms around his neck. "Yes!"

He laughed, his heart swelling against his ribs. "You're not just saying that because I'm a Super Bowl champion, are you?"

"No, I'm saying yes, because you aren't playing football anymore. You're just a rancher, and I'm going to be a rancher's wife." She leaned back with narrowed eyes. "The ranch... it's yours?"

He nodded. "Is that okay with you?"

"Yes! If it wasn't, I was thinking we'd have to buy one of our own." She smiled and lifted her face to his. "I love you, Max Smith, or Smithson, or whatever name you go by." She placed a hand against his chest. "Because I love what's inside your heart, not your bank account. And oh, by the way, I have more money than I can ever spend as well."

Max rose to his feet, bringing her with him. "We'll have to start a scholarship for future football players and models." He took the ring out of the box and slipped it onto her finger.

She held it out, admiring it on her hand. "How did you guess my size?"

"I think it was BODS."

She frowned. "I didn't put my ring size on BODS."

"No, but BODS set us up with a perfect fit. It only seemed right that the luck rubbed off on my ability to guess your ring size." He winked. "I called Leslie."

She wrapped her arms around his neck and kissed him, long and hard.

He returned the gesture, happier than he'd ever been in his life.

He needed to remember to thank Leslie and her Billionaire Online Dating Service for finding his perfect match. He would never have found Jane without the help of Leslie's genius program.

Within a week of signing up on BODS, Max was engaged to the woman who would make all his dreams come true.

"I love you, Max," Jane said.

"I love you, too, Jane," he said and kissed the tip of her nose. "Can we set a date soon?"

She nodded. "I have one request."

"That is?"

"I want you to teach me how to ride a horse before we get married."

"Then, sweetheart, let's get going." He frowned. "But why before we get married?"

"I think it would be special if we said our vows on horseback."

Max's frown deepened. "On horseback? Do you know how temperamental a horse can be around a lot of people?"

"All we need is someone to officiate, you, me, the horses and witnesses." She grinned. "I told you I was willing to learn to ride."

"Our wedding can be anything you want. We can

have monkeys hanging from the rafters, if that's what you want."

She shook her head. "No, I want to be on horseback so that I can ride into the sunset with my very own cowboy."

"Deal." He stepped back. "Grab your stuff. We're going out to the ranch. We have work to do. I don't want to wait any longer than necessary to make you mine."

EPILOGUE

FIVE YEARS LATER...

"AFTER YOU CARAMELIZE THE ONIONS, you add the garlic and sauté until the garlic is clear." Jane stirred the ingredients in the pan and looked up at the camera. "Remember nothing is exact in cooking, except the amount of love you put into the effort."

Two small, tow-headed children slammed through the back door and raced into the ranch kitchen, screaming and laughing.

"Momma, Momma, he's going to get us!" the first twin yelled.

"Slow down," Jane called out.

"Can't, or he'll eat us!" the second twin said.

"Cut!" yelled the cooking show producer.

"Sorry," Jane said. "Layne, could you round up Aurelie and Parker?" She pressed a hand to the small of her back. "Where is their father? He was supposed to be keeping them out of the kitchen while we filmed the show."

Layne scooped up Aurelie under one arm and Parker under the other. "Gotcha!"

They laughed and giggled.

Parker wiggled in Layne's grasp. "Let us down. The monster is after us."

Jane was halfway to the back door when it burst open and a six-foot-four monster, wearing a cowboy hat, charged in roaring like Sasquatch in a rage.

"Max, you're going to have those two hooligans so riled up, they'll never go down for a nap." She yanked off his cowboy hat and leaned up on her toes to kiss him.

He smiled down at her and reached out to pat her swollen belly. "I thought you weren't going to do any more shows until after the baby was born. Besides, you need to take a break and put your feet up."

"I will when I've finished the show. We only need another fifteen minutes for me to complete this episode. After that, I go on hiatus until next fall. That should give me time to get back into shape and adjust to having a third child in the house."

Max wrapped his arms around her. "I couldn't resist a chance to hold my beautiful wife." He bent to kiss her, making a loud smacking noise which made the children laugh. Then he slapped Jane lightly on the bottom, grabbed the two children from Layne and tossed them over his shoulders. "Fifteen minutes, or I'll be back to carry you out next."

Jane shook her head, smiling.

Layne's gaze followed Max and the children out of the room. Then he turned to Jane. "How do you manage them *and* a cooking show?"

"I wouldn't do it all, if I didn't love everything about my life," she said simply.

"I've never seen you happier," Layne said.

"And I've never seen you more relaxed." She gave him a pointed stare. "When are you bringing Briana and the kids out to stay with us again?"

"We have to wait until the boys are out of school for the summer. Are you sure we won't be a strain on you and Max with the new baby?"

"Briana promised to help me with the twins while I nursed the baby. I'm looking forward to seeing her again."

"I should have known you had it all figured out. You women talk."

Jane grinned. "Yes, we do. Now, if you'll let me, I have a show to finish and a husband to cuddle with before our guests arrive for dinner."

"Are you feeding them what you're cooking?"

"Oh, no. Max is grilling. I'm going to sit back with

my feet up and let him do all the work. It was our agreement when he arranged this get-together."

"Anyone I know?"

"His usual crowd, Sean, Coop, Gage, Tag and their wives."

"Is he cooking steak?" Layne asked.

"He is," Jane said, moving back to her position behind the counter. "Along with the usual hot dogs for the kids."

"I'm glad I still get to be a part of your life."

"Me, too. You're not so much my agent as a member of my family."

"Your crazy, beautiful family." Layne touched a finger to his chin. "What do you think about me and Briana buying a ranch and moving to Texas?"

"It's not for everyone," Jane said, "but I love it here, and wouldn't live anywhere else."

"You don't miss LA?"

"Never. I have everything I want and need here." She tipped her head toward the back of the room. "Let's get this filming done before my recipe spoils. I have a houseful of guests on their way and I'm not ready."

Max ducked his head back into the kitchen with the twins still over his shoulder. "Don't worry, sweetheart, I've got it all under control. All you have to do is sit and watch the master at work."

Jane laughed and threw a dishtowel in his direction. "Yeah, right. And who is going to watch the twins?"

Her life was all she'd dreamed of and more. And it would never have happened without the help of one online program called BODS.

WYATT'S WAR

HEARTS & HEROES SERIES BOOK #1

New York Times & USA Today
Bestselling Author

ELLE JAMES

New York Times & USA Today Bestselling Author

ELLE JAMES

WYATT'S

WAR

HEARTS
&
HEROES

CHAPTER 1

Sᴇʀɢᴇᴀɴᴛ Mᴀᴊᴏʀ Wʏᴀᴛᴛ Mᴀɢɴᴜs pushed past the pain in his knee, forcing himself to finish a three-mile run in the sticky heat of south Texas. Thankfully his ribs had healed and his broken fingers had mended enough he could pull the trigger again. He didn't anticipate needing to use the nine-millimeter Beretta tucked beneath his fluorescent vest. San Antonio wasn't what he'd call a hot zone. Not like Somalia, his last *real* assignment.

It wouldn't be long before his commander saw he was fit for combat duty, not playing the role of a babysitter for fat tourists, politicians and businessmen visiting the Alamo and stuffing themselves on Tex-Mex food while pretending to attend an International Trade Convention.

The scents of fajitas and salsa filled the air, accompanied by the happy cadence of a mariachi band. Twinkle lights lit the trees along the downtown River Walk as he completed his run around the San Antonio Convention Center and started back to his hotel. Neither the food, nor the music lightened his spirits.

Since being medevaced out of Somalia to San Antonio Medical Center, the combined armed forces' medical facility, he'd been chomping at the bit to get back to where the action was. But for some damn reason, his commander and the psych evaluator thought he needed to cool his heels a little longer and get his head on straight before he went back into the more volatile situations.

So what? He'd been captured and tortured by Somali militants. If he hadn't been so trusting of the men he'd been sent to train in combat techniques, he might have picked up on the signs. Staff Sergeant Dane might not be dead and Wyatt wouldn't have spent three of the worst weeks of his life held captive. He'd been tortured: nine fingers, four ribs and one kneecap broken and had been beaten to within an inch of his life. All his training, his experience in the field, the culture briefings and in-country observations hadn't prepared him for complete betrayal by the very people he had been sent there to help.

He understood why the Somali armed forces had turned him over to the residual al-Shabab militants that were attempting a comeback after being ousted from the capital, Mogadishu. He might have done the same if his family had been kidnapped and threatened with torture and beheading if he didn't hand over the foreigners.

No, he'd have found a better way to deal with the terrorists. A way that involved very painful deaths. His breathing grew shallower and the beginning of a panic attack snuck up on him like a freight train.

Focus. The psych doc had given him methods to cope with the onset of anxiety that made him feel like he was having a heart attack. He had to focus to get his mind out of Somalia and torture and back to San Antonio and the River Walk.

Ahead he spied the pert twitch of a female butt encased in hot pink running shorts and a neon green tank top. Her ass was as far from the dry terrain of Somalia as a guy could get. Wyatt focused on her and her tight buttocks, picking up the pace to catch up. She was a pretty young woman with an MP3 device strapped to her arm with wires leading to the earbuds in her ears. Her dark red hair pulled back in a loose ponytail bounced with every step. Running in *the zone*, she seemed to ignore everything around but the path in front of her.

Once he caught up, Wyatt slowed to her pace, falling in behind. His heart rate slowed, returning to normal, his breathing regular and steady. Panic attack averted, he felt more normal, in control and aware of the time. As much as he liked following the pretty woman with the pink ass and the dark red, bobbing ponytail, he needed to get back and shower before he met the coordinator of the International Trade Convention.

Wyatt lengthened his stride and passed the woman, thankful that simply by jogging ahead of him, she'd brought him back to the present and out of a near clash with the crippling anxiety he refused to let get the better of him.

As he put distance between him and the woman in pink, he passed the shadow of a building. A movement out of the corner of his eye made him spin around. He jogged in a circle, his pulse ratcheting up, his body ready, instincts on high alert. The scuffle of feet made him circle again and stop. He crouched in a fighting stance and faced the threat, the memory of his abduction exploding in his mind, slamming him back to Somalia, back to the dry terrain of Africa and the twenty rebels who'd jumped him and Dane when they'd been leading a training exercise in the bush.

Instead of Somali militants garbed in camouflage and turbans, a small child darted out of his parents' reach and ran past Wyatt, headed toward the edge of the river.

His mother screamed, "Johnnie, stop!"

By the time Wyatt grasped that the child wasn't an al-Shabab fighter, the kid had nearly reached the edge.

Wyatt lunged for the boy and grabbed him by the scruff of the neck as the little guy tripped. Johnnie would have gone headfirst into the slow-moving, shallow water had Wyatt not snagged him at the last minute.

Instead of thanking Wyatt, the kid kicked, wiggled and squirmed until Wyatt was forced to set the boy on the ground. Then Johnnie planted the tip of his shoe in Wyatt's shin with razor-sharp precision.

Wyatt released him and bent to rub the sore spot.

Little Johnnie ran back to his mother, who wrapped her arms around the brat and cooed. Safe in his mother's arms, he glared at Wyatt.

Wyatt frowned, the ache in his shin nothing compared to the way his heart raced all over again.

The boy's mother gave Wyatt an apologetic wince and hugged her baby boy to her chest. "Thank you."

A small crowd had gathered, more because Wyatt, the parents and child blocked the sidewalk than because they were interested in a man who'd just rescued a child from a potential drowning.

His heartbeat racing, his palms clammy and his pulse pounding so loudly in his ears he couldn't hear anything else, Wyatt nodded, glancing around for an escape. Fuck! What was wrong with him? If he didn't get away quickly, he'd succumb this time. Where was the woman in the pink shorts when he needed her? Some of his panic attacks had been so intense he'd actually thought he was having a heart attack. He hadn't told his commander, or the psychologist assigned to his case, for fear of setting back his reassignment even further. He wanted to be back in the field where the action was. Where he was fighting a real enemy, not himself.

As it was, he'd been given this snowbird task of heading up the security for the International Trade Convention. "Do this job, prove you're one hundred percent and we'll take it from there," Captain Ketchum had said. To Wyatt, it sounded like a load of bullshit with no promises.

Hell, any trained monkey could provide security for a bunch of businessmen. What did Ketchum think Wyatt could add to the professional security firm hired to man the exits and provide a visual deterrent to pickpockets and vagrants?

Wyatt had tried to see the assignment from his commander's point of view. He was a soldier barely recovered from a shitload of injuries caused by violent militants who set no value on life, limb and liberty. Sure, he'd been so close to death he almost prayed for it, but he was back as good as—

A twinge in his knee, made it buckle. Rather than fall in front of all those people, Wyatt swung around like he meant it and stepped out smartly.

And barreled into the woman he'd been following. Her head down, intent on moving, she'd been squeezing past him at that exact moment.

The female staggered sideways, her hands flailing in the air as she reached out to grab something to hold onto. When her fingers only met air, she toppled over the edge and fell into the river with a huge splash.

Another lady screamed and the crowd that had been standing on the sidewalk rushed to the edge of the river, pushing Wyatt forward to the point he almost went in with the woman.

A dark, wet head rose from the water like an avenging Titan, spewing curses. She pushed lank strands of hair from her face and glared up at him. "Are you just going to stand there and stare? Or are you going to get me out of this?"

Guilt and the gentleman in Wyatt urged him to hold out his hand to her. She grasped it firmly and held on as he pulled her out of the river and onto the sidewalk. She was so light, he yanked with more force than necessary and she fell against him, her tight little wet body pressing against his.

His arm rose to her waist automatically, holding her close until she was steady on her own feet.

The redhead stared up into his eyes, her own green ones wide, sparkling with anger, her pretty little mouth shaped in an O.

At this close range, Wyatt saw the freckles sprinkled across her nose. Instead of making her face appear flawed, they added to her beauty, making her more approachable, though not quite girl-next-door. She was entirely too sexy for that moniker. Especially all wet with her skin showing through the thin fabric of the lime green tank top.

Then she was pushing against him—all business and righteous anger.

A round of applause sounded behind him, though he didn't deserve it since he'd knocked her into the water in the first place. "My apologies, darlin'."

She fished the MP3 out of the strap around her arm and pressed the buttons on it, shaking her head. "Well, that one's toast."

"Sweetheart, I'll buy you a new one," Wyatt said, giving her his most charming smile. "Just give me your name and number so that I can find you to replace it."

"No thanks. I'm not your sweetheart and I don't have time to deal with it." She squeezed the water out of her hair and turned away, dropping the MP3 into a trashcan.

With her body shape imprinted in dank river water on his vest and PT shorts, he was reluctant to let her leave without finding out her name. "At least let me know your name."

She hesitated, opened her mouth to say something, then she shook her head as if thinking better of it. "Sorry, I've gotta go." She shrugged free of his grip and took off, disappearing into the throng of tourists on the River Walk.

Wyatt would have jogged after her, but the number of people on the sidewalk made it impossible for a big guy like him to ease his way through. Regret tugged at his gut. Although he hadn't made the best first impression on her, her bright green eyes and tight little body had given him the first twinge of lust he'd felt since he'd been in Somalia. Perhaps being on snowbird detail would help him get his mojo back. At the very least, he might find time, and a willing woman, to get laid. Okay, so a few days of R&R in a cushy assignment might not be too bad.

A flash of pretty green eyes haunted his every step as he wove his way through the thickening crowd to his hotel where he'd stashed his duffel bag. He wondered if in an entire city of people he'd manage to run into the red-haired jogger again. If so, maybe he could refrain from knocking her into the river next time and instead get her number.

FIONA ALLEN ARRIVED at the door to her hotel room, dripping wet and in need of a shower to rinse off the not-so-sanitary San Antonio River water. She couldn't afford to come down with some disease this week. Not when dignitaries were already arriving for the International Trade Convention due to kick off in less than two days' time.

If she did come down with something, it would all be that big, hulking, decidedly sexy, beast of a man's fault. The one who'd knocked her into the river in the first place. When he'd pulled her out with one hand, he'd barely strained.

Her heart had raced when he'd slammed her up against his chest. She blamed it on the shock of being thrown into the river, but she suspected the solid wall of muscles she'd rested her hands against had more to do with it.

For a brief moment, she'd remained dumbstruck and utterly attracted to the clumsy stranger. Had it been any other circumstance and she hadn't been covered in river slime, she might have asked for his number. *Yeah, right.*

As the convention coordinator, she couldn't afford to date or be sick, or for anything to go wrong while thousands of businessmen and politicians attended the meetings. She'd been hired by the city to ensure this event went off without a hitch, and she wouldn't let a single disgruntled employee, terrorist or hulking bodybuilder knock her off her game. No sir. She had all the plans locked up tighter than Fort Knox and the hired staff marching to the beat of her military-style drum.

She wasn't the daughter of an Army colonel for nothing. She knew discipline; hard work and using your brain couldn't be replaced by help from sexy strangers with insincere apologies. If this convention was going to be a success, it would be so based on all of her hard work in the planning stages.

Once inside her room, she headed straight for the

bathroom and twisted the knob on the shower, amazed at how much her breasts still tingled after being smashed against the broad chest of the clumsy oaf who'd knocked her into the river. She shook her head, attributing the tingling to the chill of the air conditioning unit.

In the bathroom, she stripped her damp gym shorts and tank top, dropping the soaked mess into a plastic bag. She'd hand it over to the hotel staff and ask them to launder them, otherwise she'd have nothing to work out in. Who was she kidding? She wouldn't need to work out once the convention began.

Fiona unclipped her bra and slid out of her panties, adding them to the bag of dirty clothes. Then she stepped beneath the shower's spray and attacked her body with shampoo and citrus-scented soap. Images of the muscle man on the River Walk resurfaced, teasing her body into a lather that had nothing to do with the bar of soap. Too bad her time wasn't her own. The man had certainly piqued her interest. Not that she'd find him again in a city of over a million people.

As she slid her soap-covered hand over her breast, she paused to tweak a nipple and moaned. It had been far too long since she'd been with a man. She'd have to do something about that soon. With her, a little sex went a long way. Perhaps she would test the batteries in her vibrator and make do with pleasuring herself. Although the device was cold and couldn't give her all she wanted, it was a lot less messy in so very many ways. Relationships required work. Building a business had taken all of her time.

Fiona trailed her hand down her belly to the tuft of curls over her mons and sighed. Maybe she'd find a man. After the convention when her life wasn't nearly as crazy. She rinsed, switched off the water and stepped out on the mat, her core pulsing, her clit throbbing, needy and unfulfilled.

With a lot of items still begging for her attention, she couldn't afford the luxury of standing beneath the hot spray of the massaging showerhead, masturbating. Towel in hand, she rubbed her skin briskly, her breasts tingling at the thought of the big guy on the River Walk.

By the time the convention was over, that man could be long gone. He probably was a businessman passing through, or one of the military men on temporary duty. Even if he lived in the city, what were the chances of running into him again? Slim to none. San Antonio was a big place with a lot of people.

Well, damn. She should have given him her name and number. A quick fling would get her over her lust cravings and back to her laser-sharp focus.

She dragged a brush through her long, curly hair, wishing she'd cut it all off. With the convention taking all of her spare time, she didn't have time to waste on taming her mane of cursed curls. Most of the time it was the bane of her existence, requiring almost an hour of steady work with the straightener to pull the curls out. Having left her clean clothes in the drawer in the bedroom, Fiona stood naked in front of the mirror as she blew her hair dry, coaxing it around a large round brush.

This convention was her shot at taking her business international. If she succeeded and pulled off the biggest event of her career without a hitch, other jobs would come her way on her own merit, not based on a recommendation from one of her stepfather's cronies.

When she'd graduated with her masters in Operations Management, she'd invested the money her mother had left her in her business, F.A. International Event Planner. Since then, she'd steadily built her client list from companies based in San Antonio. Starting out with weddings, parties and small gigs, she'd established a reputation for attention to detail and an ability to follow through. She'd worked her way in as a consultant for some of the larger firms in the area when they'd needed to plan a convention based in San Antonio.

Finally she'd gotten a lead on the International Trade Convention and had applied. Her stepfather put a bug in the ear of one of his buddies from his active Army days at the Pentagon and she'd landed the contract.

Now all she had to do was prove she was up to the task. If it fell apart, she'd lose her business, disgrace the U.S. government and shame her stepfather. The pressure to succeed had almost been overwhelming. To manage the workload, she'd taken out a big loan, more than doubled her staff, coordinated the use of the convention center, arranged for all the food, meeting rooms, audio-visual equipment, translators, and blocked out lodging and security for the guests.

As she dried her hair, she stared at the shadows beneath her eyes. Only a few more sleepless nights and the convention would be underway and over. She'd be playing the role of orchestra conductor, managing the staff to ensure everything was perfect. The most important aspect of the event was tight security. The Department of Homeland Security had notified her today that with all the foreign delegates scheduled to attend, the probability of a terrorist attack had risen to threat level orange.

A quick glance at her watch reminded her that she only had ten minutes to get ready before her meeting in the lounge with the man Homeland Security had insisted she add to her staff to oversee security. This last-minute addition made her nervous. She knew nothing about the man, his background or his capabilities. He could prove more of a hindrance than a help if he got in the way. All she knew was that he'd better be on time, and he'd better be good. With a hundred items roiling around in her head at any one moment, the last thing she needed was an international incident.

Fiona shut off the blow dryer, ran the brush through her hair and reached for the doorknob, reminding herself to look at the e-mail on her laptop from Homeland Security to get the name of the contact she'd be meeting shortly. Before she could turn the doorknob, it twisted in her hand and the door flew open.

A very naked man, with wild eyes and bared teeth shoved her up against the wall, pinned her wrists above her head and demanded, "Who the hell are you? And why are you in my room?"

Get Wyatt's War Here

ABOUT THE AUTHOR

ELLE JAMES also writing as MYLA JACKSON is a *New York Times* and *USA Today* Bestselling author of books including cowboys, intrigues and paranormal adventures that keep her readers on the edges of their seats. When she's not at her computer, she's traveling, snow skiing, boating, or riding her ATV, dreaming up new stories. Learn more about Elle James at www.ellejames.com

Website | Facebook | Twitter | GoodReads | Newsletter | BookBub | Amazon

Or visit her alter ego Myla Jackson at mylajackson.com
Website | Facebook | Twitter | Newsletter

Follow Me!
www.ellejames.com
ellejames@ellejames.com

ALSO BY ELLE JAMES

Hot SEAL Hawaiian Nights (SEALs in Paradise)

Brotherhood Protectors Vol 1

Hellfire Series

Hellfire, Texas (#1)

Justice Burning (#2)

Smoldering Desire (#3)

Hellfire in High Heels (#4)

Playing With Fire (#5)

Up in Flames (#6)

Total Meltdown (#7)

Declan's Defenders

Marine Force Recon (#1)

Show of Force (#2)

Full Force (#3)

Driving Force (#4)

Tactical Force (#5)

Mission: Six

One Intrepid SEAL

Two Dauntless Hearts

Three Courageous Words

Four Relentless Days

Five Ways to Surrender

Six Minutes to Midnight

Hearts & Heroes Series

Wyatt's War (#1)

Mack's Witness (#2)

Ronin's Return (#3)

Sam's Surrender (#4)

Take No Prisoners Series

SEAL's Honor (#1)

SEAL'S Desire (#2)

SEAL's Embrace (#3)

SEAL's Obsession (#4)

SEAL's Proposal (#5)

SEAL's Seduction (#6)

SEAL'S Defiance (#7)

SEAL's Deception (#8)

SEAL's Deliverance (#9)

SEAL's Ultimate Challenge (#10)

Texas Billionaire Club

Tarzan & Janine (#1)

Something To Talk About (#2)

Who's Your Daddy (#3)

Love & War (#4)

Ballistic Cowboy

Hot Combat (#1)

Hot Target (#2)

Hot Zone (#3)

Hot Velocity (#4)

Cajun Magic Mystery Series

Voodoo on the Bayou (#1)

Voodoo for Two (#2)

Deja Voodoo (#3)

Cajun Magic Mysteries Books 1-3

Billionaire Online Dating Service

The Billionaire Husband Test (#1)

The Billionaire Cinderella Test (#2)

The Billionaire Bride Test (#3)

The Billionaire Daddy Test (#4)

The Billionaire Matchmaker Test (#5)

SEAL Of My Own

Navy SEAL Survival

Navy SEAL Captive

Navy SEAL To Die For

Navy SEAL Six Pack

Devil's Shroud Series

Deadly Reckoning (#1)

Deadly Engagement (#2)

Deadly Liaisons (#3)

Deadly Allure (#4)

Deadly Obsession (#5)

Deadly Fall (#6)

Covert Cowboys Inc Series

Triggered (#1)

Taking Aim (#2)

Bodyguard Under Fire (#3)

Cowboy Resurrected (#4)

Navy SEAL Justice (#5)

Navy SEAL Newlywed (#6)

High Country Hideout (#7)

Clandestine Christmas (#8)

Thunder Horse Series

Hostage to Thunder Horse (#1)

Thunder Horse Heritage (#2)

Thunder Horse Redemption (#3)

Christmas at Thunder Horse Ranch (#4)

Demon Series

Hot Demon Nights (#1)

Protecting the Colton Bride & Colton's Cowboy Code

Heir to Murder

Secret Service Rescue

High Octane Heroes

Haunted

Engaged with the Boss

Cowboy Brigade

Time Raiders: The Whisper

Bundle of Trouble

Killer Body

Operation XOXO

An Unexpected Clue

Baby Bling

Under Suspicion, With Child

Texas-Size Secrets

Cowboy Sanctuary

Lakota Baby

Dakota Meltdown

Beneath the Texas Moon

Made in the USA
Las Vegas, NV
09 February 2024

85548226R10148